D0974584

"All right, I'll go," Julia said quietly

"But don't think it changes anything. I love you. I'm not asking you to change what you are; I'm not asking you for pretty lies. Maybe I will get hurt, but that's my risk, Hugh, not yours. You risk nothing."

He closed his eyes as if he were in pain and for a moment Julia thought she had reached him.

"No, no more, Julia." It was said with such weary bleakness that Julia retired, defeated, without another word. She left the tall, broad-shouldered man shrouded by the shadows of his room and by deeper, darker shadows that she could know nothing about. Left him brooding, alone—as he meant always to be.

WELCOME TO THE WONDERFUL WORLD OF *Harlequin Romances*

Interesting, informative and entertaining,
each Harlequin Romance portrays an appealing
and original love story. With a varied array
of settings, we may lure you on an African safari,
to a quaint Welsh village, or an exotic Riviera
location—anywhere and everywhere that adventurous
men and women fall in love.

As publishers of Harlequin Romances, we're
extremely proud of our books. Since 1949,
Harlequin Enterprises has built its publishing
reputation on the solid base of quality and
originality. Our stories are the most popular
paperback romances sold in North America; every
month, six new titles are released and sold at
nearly every book-selling store in Canada and the
United States.

For a list of all titles currently available,
send your name and address to:

HARLEQUIN READER SERVICE,
(In the U.S.) P.O. Box 52040, Phoenix, AZ 85072-2040
(In Canada) P.O. Box 2800, Postal Station A
5170 Yonge Street, Willowdale, Ont. M2N 6J3

We sincerely hope you enjoy reading
this Harlequin Romance.

Yours truly,

THE PUBLISHERS
Harlequin Romances

Love in the Valley

Susan Napier

Harlequin Books

TORONTO • NEW YORK • LONDON
AMSTERDAM • PARIS • SYDNEY • HAMBURG
STOCKHOLM • ATHENS • TOKYO • MILAN

Original hardcover edition published in 1985
by Mills & Boon Limited

ISBN 0-373-02711-7

Harlequin Romance first edition August 1985

Love is of the valley, come thou down
And find him.

Tennyson

———————◆———————

Copyright © 1985 by Susan Napier.
Philippine copyright 1985. Australian copyright 1985.
Cover illustration copyright © 1985 by Will Davies.

All rights reserved. Except for use in any review, the reproduction or utilization
of this work in whole or in part in any form by any electronic, mechanical
or other means, now known or hereafter invented, including xerography,
photocopying and recording, or in any information storage or retrieval system,
is forbidden without the permission of the publisher, Harlequin Enterprises
Limited, 225 Duncan Mill Road, Don Mills, Ontario, Canada M3B 3K9. All the
characters in this book have no existence outside the imagination of the
author and have no relation whatsoever to anyone bearing the same name
or names. They are not even distantly inspired by any individual known
or unknown to the author, and all the incidents are pure invention.

The Harlequin trademarks, consisting of the words HARLEQUIN ROMANCE
and the portrayal of a Harlequin, are trademarks of Harlequin Enterprises
Limited; the portrayal of a Harlequin is registered in the United States Patent
and Trademark Office and in the Canada Trade Marks Office.

Printed in U.S.A.

CHAPTER ONE

JULIA FRY stood back and regarded her latest creation with a certain humorous resignation. Her Cordon Bleu tutors in Paris would throw up their hands in horror at the sight of such unabashed vulgarity, but fortunately she no longer had to worry about their opinions.

'My God, what on earth is it?'

Julia turned to grin at the tall blond man who pushed through the swing doors from the hall.

'It's for tonight,' she obliged. 'My *pièce de resistance*.'

'What's it trying to resist, good taste?' As far as Phillip Randolph was concerned, lack of taste was the ultimate sin.

'Bite your tongue, Phillip,' Julia mock-scolded. 'You told me to create something special for Marcia's birthday, so I did. It'll suit her perfectly, don't you think?'

He didn't answer and they both knew why. His cousin was a shade too voluptuous, too aggressive, too just about anything to qualify in the lady stakes. Poor Phillip, Julia smiled to herself as she watched an immaculately manicured finger pass over the intricately iced patterns of flowers and leaves, she doubted that he would ever find the woman to suit his fastidious needs.

'Do you really think . . .' the finger halted and pointed stiffly, '. . . that the caterpillar is necessary?'

'How on earth did he get there!' exclaimed Julia in tones of wonderment. Brown eyes rose patiently to meet her bright, brimming blue ones and Julia sighed.

'OK.' She carefully picked the little yellow-and-green iced object off a curling green leaf. 'I thought you might have overlooked him. He's rather cute, don't you think?'

'No,' replied her employer bluntly. 'You haven't hidden a spider anywhere too, have you? Amongst the foliage?'

'I was tempted, but I resisted,' Julia giggled into his suspicious face.

'You amaze me,' replied Phillip drily, straightening up and flicking a non-existent speck from the sleeve of his beautifully tailored suit.

That about summed up their relationship, mused Julia as she watched him preen. She was constantly having to resist the urge to puncture his self-conscious dignity, while on his part he found her sense of humour and frankness disconcerting to say the least.

'You still haven't told me exactly what it is.' He stroked his well-clipped moustache absently.

'It's a bombe. A very spectacular bombe,' said Julia modestly.

'What does it do—go off in our mouths?'

'Something like that,' agreed Julia. 'There's enough brandy in there to stun an elephant . . . or at least to slow Marcia's mouth down from seventy-eight to thirty-three-and-a-third.'

'Jealous?' jeered Phillip slyly.

'Rabidly,' was the cheerfully insincere reply. Rich, still single in his mid-thirties and a prominent member of New Zealand's business and social community, Phillip was used to being regarded in a flattering light, particularly by women. Julia saw it almost as a duty to try and stop the rot.

'Half the time I never know whether you're joking or not,' Phillip complained as Julia placed the platter holding the bombe into the double-doored refrigerator. 'Don't you fancy me at all?'

'What a vulgar turn of phrase,' said Julia mischievously. And at his pained look: 'Well of course I fancy you, you're very fanciable. But you're not my type.'

'What *is* your type?'

Julia considered it briefly. 'Someone who laughs a

lot, who can make me laugh. Dark, handsome . . . and, of course, short!' At five foot and half an inch, height was a tender subject with Julia.

'In other words, a Latin hysteric,' said Phillip sourly and Julia giggled.

'Right! And while you're away I'll have some time to look around for him.' Phillip was off on yet another of his overseas business trips.

'Haven't you got any work lined up?' Phillip asked.

'Not yet. But there's plenty of time. You don't leave until next month.' When he was away for longer than four weeks Phillip usually paid her a retainer so that she was free to find outside work temporarily if she wished. With her reputation she could pick and choose her jobs.

'July twenty-first,' he confirmed. 'But I *have* heard of something for you, if you're interested.'

'What?' asked Julia, without much hope.

'The Marlows,' he said, sounding insufferably smug.

Julia let out a whoop of delight as she turned on him. 'I don't believe it! Where? When?'

'At Craemar, in August, for a month. I thought you'd be pleased.'

'How did you come to hear?'

'I met Constance last week at the theatre and happened to mention I was going away.'

'Why didn't you tell me!' Julia hoped no one else had got the job in the interim.

'I forgot,' admitted Phillip with irritating calmness. He could be selfishly casual when his own well-being wasn't involved. 'She wants you to ring her about it.' He shot back a pristine cuff. 'I must go. No lunch today, Julia, but there'll be six tomorrow.' He often entertained during the day as well as in the evenings, so Julia never lacked for variety of challenge.

She turned back to the cluttered bench as he left, wondering about the Marlows. They usually went down to their holiday home on the Coromandel Peninsula at Christmas, not in the dead of winter. Julia had worked for them once before at Craemar, two Christmasses ago, helping their resident cook/housekeeper to cater for an extended family reunion. It had been hard work, but fun.

Constance Marlow was one of New Zealand's best-loved actresses and her husband, Michael, a leading stage director and playwright. Their children were almost all involved in the arts in one field or another, making a name for themselves in their own rights.

Her curiosity growing by the minute, Julia washed her hands and used the yellow kitchen phone to call Constance and make an appointment to see her the next day. That done she dedicated herself to preparing an elegant birthday dinner to precede the bombe.

The next morning, success confirmed by Phillip's unqualified approval over breakfast, Julia drove her battered little VW the few miles to the Marlows' Remuera town house. Getting no answer from the front door, she strolled around the back to find Constance sitting in the weak autumn sunshine beside the pool, studying the typed pages of a script. Julia had not seen her at close quarters for a year, although she had been to several of her plays, but Constance looked as slim, as vital as she did on stage, the glorious red hair swept up into a knot of fire, the green eyes sparkling with life.

'Julia!' Lovely to see you again,' she cried, in liquid tones. 'Sit down on one of these loungers and enjoy the sun. We're not going to have it for long by the look of those clouds. I'm glad you've arrived, this thing was beginning to drive me mad with boredom.' She threw the offending pages on to the manicured grass.

'A new play, Mrs Marlow?' asked Julia, smilingly taking a seat.

'TV script, and do call me Connie—I told you that last time. Otherwise I shall start feeling really decrepit.'

'You're looking as young as ever,' responded Julia, instantly put at her ease.

'Thanks, I needed that,' Connie laughed with the

confidence of one who knew it was the truth. 'Forty-
nine I was last week, and do you know what that
wretch Richard offered me for my birthday—a face-
lift!'

Julia watched in amusement as Connie described the
gifts she had received from her family with extravagant
gestures of the graceful hands. It was incredible to
think, looking at Connie's willowy grace, that she was
the mother of six children, including two sets of twins.
Incredible too, that one so volatile and apparently
disorganised could be the lynch pin of the family, but
matriarch was a role Connie enjoyed playing to the full,
when she got the chance.

'Well, are you coming down to Craemar with us? We
really need you and it won't be too onerous. There'll
only be us, this time, not all the aunts and cousins. Not
Hugh, of course,' she added as an afterthought. Julia
had never met the mysterious Hugh. He was the eldest
son, older than Julia, a lawyer who seemed to steer well
clear of the rest of the family's flamboyancy.

'Aren't you going down at Christmas?' asked Julia
curiously.

Connie sighed. 'I'm afraid tradition has to give way
to expediency this year, we'll all be scattered to the
winds at Christmas.' She began counting off her fingers.
'Michael will be directing me in a play at Downstage in
Wellington—one of his own incidentally, he'll be
working on it at Craemar so bear with him won't you?
Richard has a part in a film that's going on location to
Easter Island. Steven is scheduled to tour Japan.
Rosalind is going to try her luck on the London stage,
God help her! Olivia is still wrapped up in that artists'
commune and they're having an exhibition and Charles,
Charles wants to go and stay with a friend at Taupo.
My baby—wants to be away at Christmas!'

Julia hid a smile. Charley, Charles only to Connie,
was the extreme tail-ender of the family. Only fourteen
and still at boarding school he was the only Marlow

child who didn't have red hair. He was a solemn but likeable boy, rather quiet, and Connie was at a bit of a loss with him. She loved him as much as she loved the others, but she felt she didn't understand him. 'Generation gap yawning at me,' she had once said to Julia.

'I suppose it won't be the same as having Christmas, or are you going to have presents and a tree?' Julia grinned.

'It'll be bloody cold for a start,' Connie said forcefully. 'But we can have lots of fires—I love fires, don't you? Central heating's so soulless. And I refuse to be done out of the little time we have every year to be together as a real family. I had to brow-beat the lot of them; threaten to *kidnap* Steven but I refuse to be deprived. Charles is getting out of school a week early and we'll have an entire month. Could you stand us for that long?'

'I'd love it,' said Julia warmly. 'But surely Mrs Brabbage could cope if it's just family.'

'Housekeeping's her limit at the moment,' Connie's voice softened in affection. 'She finally persuaded that stubborn husband of hers to have his hip operation. He's out of the hospital but still not very mobile, and won't be for a while yet. Jean will come in every day to do a bit of cleaning—"to take her out of herself" as she puts it—but she won't be able to cook for us. Hence you!'

'Thanks for thinking of me,' said Julia, feeling sorry for Jack Brabbage. He was a tiny, wiry man, in contrast to his massive wife, and the sort who would jibe at a long period of inactivity. 'Or wasn't I first choice?'

Connie gave her a look of wide-eyed innocence, then laughed, the clear, joyous sound that was her trademark. 'Actually I hadn't anyone in mind until I saw Phillip on opening night. When he told me he was going away it was like a sign from the gods.'

'I'm sorry I didn't ring you straight away, but he didn't tell me about the offer until yesterday.'

'Don't worry about it,' Connie shrugged her apology away, 'I know how these businessmen are. And don't worry that you might get snowed under with work, I've issued dire threats to anyone who turns up with hangers-on. *And* I've told everyone to keep their mouths shut, a necessity these days I'm afraid.' She displayed a gamine grin. 'Richard and Ros have collected quite a fan club over these television series of theirs, and Steven is constantly pursued by weirdos— pink hair and safety pins, and that's only the boys!' The last was said on a rising note of outrage but the green eyes glittered like jewels in amusement. Connie had the broadmindedness of her profession and in her case this extended to a patient and generous tolerance of all except the most unrepentantly evil people.

'Pursuit is an occupational hazard for rock stars,' Julia replied in the same vein. 'I seem to remember *you* with safety pins and pink hair at one time.'

'That was acting darling, these people are real life. Anyway, you agree then, do you?' Connie named a very fair figure and Julia nodded. 'Believe me, darling, you'll earn every penny, the family is bigger and hungrier than ever. You should see Charles now, he's getting on for six foot! He was in the school play this term, you know. Has the makings of a fine actor. I thought I might see if Michael can pull some strings while we're down in Wellington and get him an audition at the Drama School.' This was all said on one breath but it was Julia, not Connie, who was left gasping.

They discussed terms and Julia agreed to travel down to Craemar a few days ahead of the family to prepare for their arrival. The nearest store was quite a distance from the bush-clad valley in which Craemar nestled so there would be no nipping out to the shops if she ran out of anything essential.

'Now business is settled, why don't we go inside and

get a cup of coffee?' suggested Connie, looking up at the lowering sky. 'I think it's going to rain at any moment.'

They reached the french doors of the lounge just as the torrent began and Julia brushed off the heavy drops before settling comfortably on the sagging grey couch. While Connie fetched the coffee Julia looked around the slightly shabby room. It was a very much lived-in room, the kind that Julia felt at home in.

'Julia Fry, by all that's holy! Light of my life, where have you been hiding these last few months?'

'Hello, Richard,' Julia jumped up to offer a light kiss, and receive an enthusiastic one in exchange from the tall, handsome, red-headed young man who had materialised before her. He dropped beside her on the couch and threw an arm over her shoulder.

'You're looking ravishing, sweetheart. Coming to slave for us are you?'

'I couldn't resist the chance to be close to my favourite TV star,' Julia batted her eyelashes at him and they grinned at each other. She had known Richard on and off since they had met in London, Julia working as a cook at the New Zealand embassy and Richard going to RADA. They had the kind of friendship that survived gaps of months, even years, in which they never saw each other. 'I hear you've made it to the big time. Which crowd scene are you going to be in? Or have you actually got a speaking part in this movie?'

'Wretch!' howled Richard. 'It's the lead, as well you know. And what about my Festival coup, aren't you going to congratulate me on that?'

'I think you'll make a fantastic Romeo,' she said sincerely, having read about it in the papers.

'With Dad directing I couldn't really miss, could I,' said Richard modestly. Both of them knew that Michael Marlow was ruthless as a director; nepotism didn't get a look in. On the other hand he didn't give a damn about rumours of favouritism, if his son was the best for the part, it was his.

'And Connie's playing the nurse. How come Ros wasn't picked for Juliet?'

'That would have been a bit *too* incestuous.' He winked, 'Besides, Dad's discovered this perfect gem of a sixteen-year-old. Gorgeous little thing, and madly in love with me, of course,' he hammed outrageously.

'Aren't we all.' Richard's ridiculous megastar act never failed to bring Julia out in the giggles.

'I thought I heard sounds of violent over-acting.' Connie entered carrying a tray with three cups on it. 'Don't you have a rehearsal this morning, young man?' Richard was currently on stage, doing readings of seventeenth-century poetry.

'They let me off for good behaviour. I'm free to autograph a fan or two.' He ruffled Julia's blonde, shoulder-length curls and leered wickedly at her.

Julia sipped her coffee and listened to the by-play between mother and son, wondering why she had never fallen in love with Richard. She had certainly had the time and opportunity, and he was extremely attractive. Lack of challenge, perhaps? Or the conviction that a sudden, tempestuous love awaited her somewhere?

'Why didn't you come backstage and see me!' cried Richard, on learning that Julia had seen his current production.

'Couldn't be bothered fighting my way through the panting hordes at the stage door,' said Julia mildly.

'Isn't it incredible,' agreed his mother. 'If only they knew what a moody, slovenly, emotionally immature beast he was, they'd be fighting to get away.'

'They fill the seats, Mama, they fill the seats. Now, why don't you go back to that turgid drama you're angling for a part in, and I'll see if I can persuade Julia to eat with me.'

'Sorry, other plans,' Julia said coolly and Connie laughed.

'Keep it up, darling. Having you around for a month is going to be handy in controlling that puff-ball ego of his.' She rose and gathered up her script, ordering imperiously. 'You may see to the cups, Richard, it might give your hands something *else* to do.'

A little later, having helped Richard with the few dishes, Julia peered out the window.

'Has it stopped raining yet? I really must be going.'

She was whirled into a close embrace. 'Don't run away, my darling! Don't try and fight this thing between us. Come back to my flat and have a jug of wine and a loaf of bread with me.'

'No thanks, I've meals to cook ... and this thing between us is a damp towel. Let me go, Richard, I can't breathe!' Richard wasn't broad but he was tall and Julia's face was buried in his chest.

He released her, chanting mournfully:

> ' "I burne and cruell you, in vaine
> Hope to quench me with disdaine." '

Julia was unimpressed, having heard him use exactly the same quotation before an audience of several hundred a few weeks before. Still, he did have a beautiful way with words. In spite of her striving to be practical, Julia possessed a strong streak of romanticism that was constantly getting in the way. Perhaps *that* was why she hadn't fallen in love with Richard, he was too free with something she considered should be private and special between two people.

'Oh well,' he wasn't discouraged. 'I'll have you at my mercy in August.'

'You and the rest of the family,' Julia pointed out.

'Mmmm.' He paused, his hand on the door-knob. 'Have you seen Steve lately?'

Julia shook her head and he frowned. 'Nor have I, not since before his Australian tour. If it wasn't so silly I'd say he was trying to avoid me. He didn't look too wonderful.'

'What's the matter?' Julia tried to remember the last time she had seen his twin perform. It was on a local television show. The group, *Hard Times*, was excellent, but it was Steve's distinctive voice as a lead singer that lifted them into chart-topping ranks. It had a harsh, gravelly quality, very attractive, very sexy. Julia had thought Steve looked thin and his red hair had accentuated his pallor, but it was a look he had cultivated.

'I don't know,' Richard answered. 'I don't think he was looking forward to the tour, for one thing, although he didn't say so. He and the group have been pretty constantly on the road for a couple of years now, and there's been a bit of disagreement. Steve seemed very edgy . . . uptight.'

'Maybe a month of peace and quiet in Coromandel is just what he needs, then,' said Julia, as they walked down the rain-slick driveway to her car. To her surprise, Richard, after a moment, began to laugh.

'I was just thinking,' he explained, seeing her puzzlement, 'peace and quiet . . . that's one thing a certain member of the family is going to find elusive down there.'

'You mean your father, with his writing?'

'No, no . . .' Richard looked furtively over his shoulder. 'Hugh!'

'I don't understand.'

Richard was grinning widely. 'He's going to be down at Craemar with the rest of us.'

'But Connie said he wouldn't be. I thought he didn't like family get-togethers.'

'He doesn't know! He's been over in America doing some legal research. He doesn't know that Mother darling, in her infinite wisdom, has disorganised us all with her plans. He's writing this legal text-book you see, for the university—he lectures there sometimes—and he's decided to do it all in one go, without distractions . . . at Craemar. He's burnt his boats quite thoroughly by letting his apartment to a visiting American professor and his family and he won't be able to come back up to the town house because Connie's having the decorators in with a vengeance while we're away. What a gory, glorious scene it's going to be!'

Julia, usually attuned to Richard's sense of humour, and tolerant of his practical jokes, was at a loss. 'I don't see what's so funny.'

'You don't know Hugh! Individually he likes us, but he needs a good few months' notice to psyche himself up to endure the family *en masse*. Our Hugh is not a social animal, why, even at Christmas he can only stand us for a few days.'

'Maybe he gets enough excitement in his work,' said Julia, doubtful of this unlikely sounding Marlow. 'Lawyers must have to socialise with every man and his dog.'

'Ah, but then he's not *your* kind of legal eagle, darling,' Richard explained with a grin. 'He's not a blood and guts and "where were you on the night of the thirty-first" lawyer. He's a party-of-the-first-part lawyer, a dry-as-dust commercial lawyer. Nothing so untidy and unreliable as human emotion for our Hugh.'

Julia felt a tug of curiosity. 'Don't you like him?'

'Of course I like him . . . love him come to that. He's one of us, don't mistake me. When we were kids he was the story-teller, the adjudicator in all our fights, and being so much older than the rest of us we were a bit in awe of him. That was where the rot started, I think. We respected his privacy too much, let him retreat to the fringes of our lives as we grew older, instead of getting to know him better. And now he's out of reach . . . almost. When I get the chance I like to remind him who he is and what he's part of. I can't resist giving him the occasional provocative prod—and August will be more than that, it'll be a whacking great thump over the head!'

'You're really enjoying this aren't you?' murmured Julia, unable to get a clear picture of the man Richard was describing. He sounded rather dull . . . commercial law, for goodness sake! Julia had always pictured him as a kind of red-headed Perry Mason in the past, now she hastily toned it down. But a dull Marlow? It was a contradiction in terms.

'Loving every delicious moment,' admitted Richard unrepentantly. 'I can't wait to see his impotent squirming when Connie gets hold of him. She'll not let him escape our clutches—he may be impatient of the rest of us, but Connie he won't refuse, not categorically anyway. I was over at his place, you know, when this American professor phoned and let the cat out of the bag. Hugh swore me to eternal silence so silent I shall remain! I nearly killed myself driving home, I was laughing so hard.'

He was still laughing as Julia drove away and she briefly entertained the thought that it might be something of a strain to survive Richard's practical jokes day in, day out. Poor Hugh. She hoped he was equal to the shock.

CHAPTER TWO

OVER the weeks leading up to and following Phillip's departure, Julia saw quite a lot of Richard Marlow. Declaring himself in need of intelligent female companionship he set himself the task of taking over Julia's social life. He was great company, if a trifle exhausting and his presence was like a blast of fresh air in Julia's life. If now and then he lapsed into moodiness she put it down to actor's temperament. Had it been any other man, she might have thought that the desire for her constant company was a sign that he was beginning to get serious. But Richard never got serious about any women.

When he told her that he was going down to Craemar the weekend before Julia, baching it for a few days, her impulsive generosity surfaced and she promised to make up one of her special hampers for him. His instant acceptance left her with the feeling that her too-ready sympathies had been very cleverly manipulated.

When he collected his bounty on the Friday, Richard was wildly over-effusive with his thanks, handing over a fistful of dollars to cover her expenses and cheerfully informing her that his chief duty was to get to Craemar before his elder brother.

'I want to be there when The Man meets his fate!' he cried as the dusty MG took off with a callous roar, scattering gravel from Phillip's well-raked driveway as he took the curve at speed. Really, he was a shocking driver, thought Julia as she prepared for her own journey. She was spending the weekend with her parents at Ngatea, a handy stop-over on the way to Craemar.

20

Julia had lived independently of her parents ever since she had left New Zealand at eighteen to further her experience in Europe. But her family background had been a happy and secure one and she had always kept in close touch, wherever her life took her.

Arriving at Ngatea in time for morning tea, Julia found herself subjected to the usual parental interrogation about her health and welfare, and, naturally, her current lack of a steady boyfriend.

'When I think of all those nice boys you used to bring home,' her mother sighed reminiscently, 'and all those *interesting* European men you wrote home about ... wasn't there even *one* ...?'

'Nope.' Julia helped herself to another piece of shortbread, wishing absently that she had inherited her mother's fine-boned figure. Instead she had her father's sturdy genes. She was the same height as her mother, but more generously endowed in all directions. As a teenager she had agonised about the embarrassing lushness of her lines, compared to the coltish modesty of her schoolmates'.

'I don't suppose you and Richard Marlow ...?' Nan Fry began wistfully.

'Nope.' Julia rolled her eyes at her father, and he came obligingly to the rescue.

'Oh, leave her alone, Nan. Give her a few years yet. Remember, *we* didn't meet until we were thirty. I'd rather Julia was too much discriminating than too little.'

Was she too discriminating? Julia wondered that night as she settled into the familiar sag of her narrow bed. Her friends all seemed to fall in and out of love at the drop of a hat. She was sure none of *them* were still virgins.

The trouble was that she had never been severely tempted, not even by some of the suave operators she had met in Europe. She had never yet met a man who made her breathless, who made her heart pound, who thrilled her with his touch, the kind of unmistakable signs that her friends talked about. Oh, she had had great fun with a number of men—laughed, talked, petted a little, but had never felt any compelling curiosity to carry it further. She couldn't believe that all there was to love was liking someone enough to fall into bed with them.

Julia's weekend passed with leisured slowness, interrupted only by the noisy arrival of her brother, Ben, on his motorcycle. Skinny, bearded, and going through a laconic phase, he mellowed with the roast lamb, sloughing the veneer currently favoured by his university peers.

'How's life, Julia Jinx?' he asked, through a mouthful of roast potato.

'She offered to mow the lawns yesterday afternoon,' Edward Fry told him tolerantly.

'Don't tell me . . . the engine blew up!'

'Close,' his father grinned. 'A wheel fell off.'

Ben gave a shout of laughter and Julia glared at him. Her hopelessness with things mechanical was a family joke. Automatic washing machines, copiers, vacuum cleaners and even electronic games behaved mysteriously when she attempted to operate them. That's why she stuck so determinedly to her rust-bucket of a VW. It wasn't new and shiny and sophisticated; and potentially lethal! The only other piece of machinery she trusted was her second-hand blender. She had bought it from a London flatmate who had originally purchased it in the Middle East. It had an indistinguishable brand name and made a horrific noise when it worked, but it did work. 'Buster' Julia affectionately called her miracle and it was in her car now, resting reverently in her suitcase along with her very expensive set of German chef's knives and the weighty cookery tome that was her Bible.

Julia had intended to leave early Sunday afternoon, but her little break had made her lazy and it was nearly four o'clock before she threw her overnight bag into the front seat of her car and said goodbye to her parents.

Ben gave her a brotherly once-over. Julia's pint-sized figure was clad in a warm but shrunken sweatshirt, bearing the legend: Conserve Our Wildlife ... Love a Kiwi. Black leather jacket and matching jeans and cowboy boots completed the picture. For convenience she had bunched her flyaway curls into short pigtails and several recalcitrant freckles stood out prominently on her scrubbed cheeks.

'You look like a pre-adolescent bikie. Want to borrow my wheels?'

Julia wrinkled her nose. 'You should be so lucky. I know you're just jealous of my eternal youth.'

It wasn't only her lack of inches that made her look young. The largeness of the deep blue eyes fringed with thick, light brown lashes made the rest of her small, oval face look oddly babyish, as if it still had to grow to adult size.

Julia hummed and sang as she drove, glad she had worn her leathers as the afternoon grew colder, and her heater failed to function. From Thames she took the west coast road to Tapu, where she turned off on to route 29, which would take her across the Coromandel Ranges to the eastern side of the narrow peninsula.

As the little Beetle laboured up the narrow twisting road from Tapu the scenery began to change from farmland and regenerated scrub to a proud, natural wilderness. Here the native rainforest grew thick and green, spreading a protective canopy over the land, providing a refuge for some of New Zealand's rarer birds and animals. Even Julia, who was essentially a city girl at heart, felt the impact of its awesome beauty.

She seemed to be the only car on the road, which was a blessing since her speed was negligible on the slopes. The bush dropped unnervingly away from the edge of the road, down into the deep foliage of the gullies. Rimu, Totara, Kahikatea, Rata and Kauri, all prized for their timber, grew straight and tall on the ridges, protected from exploitation by their inaccessibility. The road seemed to be a puny attempt by man to impose himself on nature but at least it was sealed, and well marked, thought Julia as she carefully rounded another corner.

Coming over the top of another stomach-churning rise something caught Julia's eye in her rear-view mirror and she gasped out loud. A great, gleaming grey monster had slunk up behind her. Low-slung and dangerous it was gaining on her rapidly. It must slow down, realised Julia looking at the road ahead, there would be nowhere safe for him to pass for a few more bends yet, all uphill. It had to be a him, women didn't seem to feel the same need to prove themselves on the road that men did.

He did slow down, but not enough. He came annoyingly close, snapping at her heels and stayed there through several curves, obviously expecting her to pull over and let him pass. He needed a lesson in manners whoever he was—some flashy young buck with more money than he knew what to do with! She didn't know what the car was, but it was foreign and expensive.

Suddenly there was a feathery flash in front of her bonnet and instinctively, foolishly, Julia put her foot on the brake and swerved slightly. The Beetle practically stopped dead and to her disbelief Julia felt a distinct bump at her rear. The idiot had actually hit her!

Julia groaned as she pulled the car over on to a narrow shoulder. She was suffering an acute attack of the guilts—she should have let him pass, instead of boorishly hogging the road with her decrepit machine. However he, being at the rear, was the one who would be at fault in law, Julia was sure, and she wasn't about to allow herself to be talked into taking the blame. She only hoped he wasn't too mad.

She sneaked a look in her peeling wing mirror and saw the grey car crouched behind her. A door opened and a silver head poked out. She relaxed slightly. An elderly man—a wealthy old gentleman who was unlikely to offer physical violence. She wound down her window, drawing in a breath at the sharpness of the air. It had an edge, a purity, that you didn't find in the city.

Her hand froze on the handle as she saw the head go up as the man pushed himself up out of the car . . . and up, and up, and up . . . Goodness—he was a giant! Broad and tall he came striding towards her as though he wore seven-league boots. He wasn't elderly either. As he got closer, filling her mirror, she could see that he was only in his thirties, the deceptive grey hair was prematurely so.

The incredible hulk reached her and bent down to her window. His eyes were grey too, grey and cold and she waited for the blast of ice from the voice.

'Are you all right?'

She stared. His voice was soft and deep, almost gentle. She looked at him suspiciously. Maybe he was a psychopath on the loose. Men were usually so touchy about their cars and here he was sounding as if he was just passing the time of day with her.

'Yes.' Her voice squeaked and she coughed. 'Are you?'

'Shall we look at the damage?'

It was a clear invitation for her to step out of the car but she hesitated as he straightened and she caught sight of the hands hanging loosely by his sides. They matched the rest of him for size. She swallowed, then looked back at the grey car and was reassured by its luxuriousness.

She got out of the car, wishing her boots had a few inches more heel. Why, she only came up to his chest! She was even more determined not to be intimidated. She marched around to the front of his car and closed her eyes briefly at its pristine, untouched beauty. The curving black bumper gripped in the mouth of the monster had nary a scratch. The blinkered bonnet sloped down to a silver trident logo—a Maserati; they cost well into six figures Julia remembered from a magazine article, no wonder the man didn't seem too concerned about a minor bump, all his troubles must be padded with money.

The Beetle had come out of the encounter the worse, though only the bumper was dented. The Hulk went down on his haunches and inspected the damage. Standing behind him Julia was presented with an acre of broad back covered with impeccable Harris Tweed. The trousers were tweed too, and the plain brown leather shoes screamed Italy. Julia, who didn't have an envious bone in her body nonetheless felt peeved about his calmness.

'You were following too closely you know,' she stated firmly.

'Fortunately there's not much damage,' the soft voice replied. 'The car is insured, I presume?'

'Yes. But it's not *my* insurance company that's going to have to pay out.'

He stood up, surveyed her steadily. She waited for the denial, the defence, but it didn't come. Instead he reached into the inside pocket of his jacket and produced a pen and a square business card. He turned it over and wrote on the back, supporting the card on a broad palm.

Taking the hint Julia went back to the open door of the VW and rummaged in her shoulder bag. She scribbled her name and address and the name of her insurance company on a torn-off scrap of perfumed pink notepaper. Her hand shook slightly and she frowned. The accident must have given her more of a shock than she'd thought. She backed out of the car and came up against a solid tweed wall.

'Sorry,' she thrust her piece of paper at him and accepted the card. G. B. H. Walton said the strong black type on matt white and Julia was transfixed by the initials. What did they stand for—Grievous Bodily

Harm? She giggled.

'Accidents amuse you?' Again the soft, slow voice, unnerving from such a tough-looking individual. He didn't sound surprised, he had probably judged her by the leathers; mis-judged her rather, Julia thought.

'Oh no, no,' Julia wiped the smile off her face and sought for something else to say. Unfortunately she said the first thing that came into her mind. 'You're so big!' Stupid. Now he would say something condescending about her size.

'I know.' He slowly perused the paper in his hand, then put the scrap in his pocket. Everything about the man was measured, as if he had to consider every movement in terms of weight displacement.

'I shall say it was your fault on the form,' Julia told him in a final attempt to get him to comment on the accident.

He inclined his head slightly and held the car door for her. Julia gave up and subsided into the seat.

'See you in court,' she said impishly. It was a nice exit line but there was no exit. Five minutes later, after staring at the incomprehensible workings under the bonnet she glared at the silent watcher.

'Why don't you offer to help?'

'I'm not a mechanic. Are you a member of the AA?' He seemed to expect a negative answer, and he got one.

'Well, what do you suggest?' Julia asked, staring him in the eye, leaving him in no doubt as to what *she* suggested.

'Will the nearest petrol station do?'

'It'll have to, won't it,' snapped Julia. Honestly, he had no need to sound so reluctant. She couldn't help adding: 'And I promise I won't mug you on the way.'

He didn't deign to answer that. He helped her carry her bags to the Maserati and slung them easily into the front boot. Julia had never been within touching distance of such an elegant vehicle. She sank into the soft leather of the passenger seat and the door shut with a solid clunk. The Hulk slid in beside her and the engine purred to life at a touch, the merest throb of sound behind her head. The interior was beautifully warm and Julia shrugged out of her jacket before she fastened the retracting seatbelt.

'What is it?' she murmured, eyes wandering over the impressive dash. 'I mean, I know it's a Maserati of some kind.'

'Bora.' The wheel slid through the large hands as they gained speed. It was like gliding. If she hadn't looked out of the window Julia wouldn't have known they were going uphill or following more tortuous curves. There was no squealing of tyres or sideways drift, just smooth power.

'What does it do?' she asked.

'Everything.'

'I mean, what speed?'

He didn't take his eyes off the road. 'Are you really interested?'

'I'm interested in everything,' said Julia truthfully.

'Allright. It's a four-thousand-seven-hundred-and-nineteen cc V8 with quadruple overhead camshafts and four Weber carburettors. It develops three-hundred-and-thirty five bhp at six-thousand rpm. Top speed over two-hundred-and-seventy kph.'

'Oh.' Julia absorbed the double-Dutch. 'How fast have you gone in her?'

'Fast enough.'

Julia sighed. 'I'm not an undercover cop, you know. I only asked.'

'One-hundred-and-sixty kph.'

'What did it feel like?' she asked curiously. She couldn't imagine him getting a thrill out of speed, or anything else for that matter. Too stolid.

'Interesting.'

She laughed, turning in her seat to study him. What a challenge he presented. She would love to make him smile, get him to show a bit of animation in that poker face. People revealed themselves in smiles, in what they smiled at. To Julia it was a natural condition.

There was a lot of him to reveal. The car was a two-seater, both of them pushed well back but while Julia's legs kicked into space, her companion's flexed easily at the pedals. He must be six foot four at least, she decided, and if it wasn't for the fact that she didn't go for big men she could find him quite attractive. His face was strong-boned and square-jawed, the heavy-lidded eyes rimmed with dark brown lashes and topped with heavy dark brows. Perhaps his hair had once been dark brown too but there was no trace of it now, it was completely grey, trimmed stylishly short, and very straight. His skin was very pale and smooth, with very few lines to mar it, almost like a mask. Julia wondered what the man behind it was really like.

'You never even asked why I put my brakes on,' she said at last. 'Aren't you interested to know what made you crash into me?'

'I know already.' He continued, conversationally, 'And did *you* know that Mynahs are an introduced bird? Their numbers are reaching nuisance proportions, at expense of our native species.'

Julia's jaw dropped at the callous attitude. 'You mean that the world might be better off if I flattened a few with my car,' she said hotly. 'Well, I'm sorry, but I don't like killing anything, nuisance or not. For that matter you might say the same of people!'

To her satisfaction he seemed momentarily startled. 'You have a point,' he murmured. 'But if the crunch came, I hope you'd choose men over Mynahs.'

'The crunch did come, owing to your poor driving,' Julia needled, unwilling to accede that he, too, had a point. But her innate honesty impelled her to say, grumpily, 'Maybe it was dumb, but it was a split-second reaction. It didn't occur to me just to run the poor thing down.'

'Do your parents know where you are?'

The sudden question stumped her for a moment until

she realised his mistake. She grinned to herself. Ben had
hit the nail on the head with his description of her
appearance. Though her youthful appearance annoyed
her on occasion, like when men treated her over-
protectively, or condescendingly, it had advantages too.
It gave her the element of surprise. The 'small body,
small mind' brigade were usually shocked to find that
the pretty blonde doll wasn't as gullible as she looked.
Perhaps this man thought that he could get away with
blaming her inexperience for the accident.

'Of course they know where I am,' she said airily. 'I
do have a licence, if that's what you're thinking. I am
over sixteen you know.'

'I'm sure you are.' They had hit a straight and the
grey eyes briefly left the road. They ran from her cheeky
expression down over the firm, bouncy outline of her
breasts against the tight sweatshirt to the curvaceous
thighs encased in black leather.

'Do you like what you see?' she said, provocatively.

'I see a little girl, playing at being adult,' he said
dampeningly and she grinned at the stern profile. The
mix of innocent face and deliciously adult curves always
got to the disapproving ones.

'Good game, though,' she agreed. 'Plenty of scope for
advancement. What do you do?' She wanted to confirm
her theory that he was something solidly professional
and eminently respectable, banker or accountant, or
maybe even a doctor.

'I work,' he said, the implication clear.

'So do I,' Julia told him. 'I'm not on the dole, you
know. Though I am ... er ... in between jobs at the
moment.' Literally.

'What do you do?' Heavens, another question! He
must be cracking under the conversational strain.

'Domestic work,' she deliberately downgraded herself.
'I like it but my employers keep making improper
suggestions.'

'That doesn't surprise me, if you go around dressed

like that.'

'Oh, I never wear a bra,' Julia revealed wickedly, guessing the direction of his thoughts. 'They're so confining!'

'Well then, you can hardly be shocked when the master reacts accordingly.'

'Oh, I don't mind really, if they're nice,' the blush-making sentiment came out unblushingly. It seemed that *he* was as gullible as *she* looked!

'And what do your parents think of all this?'

'I don't tell them, they'd just get uptight about it. They're a bit old-fashioned.' Like myself, thought Julia, tired of baiting the poor man. Her mouth had run away with her as usual. She was just about to tell him her real age and profession when he said, with undisguised boredom:

'Interesting as I find this discussion of modern morality, would you mind if we listened to some music?' He didn't wait for a reply but reached forward and snapped a tape into the sophisticated radio-cassette player. Music instantly poured forth from the door mounted speakers, classical and lyrically beautiful, even to Julia's untutored ears.

'What is it?' she asked, raising her voice slightly.

'Mahler's First Symphony,' she was told, tersely. 'Listen.'

And shut up, added Julia silently. Oh well, so be it. She settled back in the seat and closed her eyes, letting the music flow over her. She didn't understand it but, surprisingly, liked it.

She didn't open her eyes again until she felt the car slow down and come smoothly to a halt a quarter of an hour later. They were at a petrol station which had a small panel-beating yard attached. The Hulk swung himself out of the car with an ease that belied his size and Julia too scrambled out. As though he thought she was incapable, her companion calmly took charge, explaining her predicament to the friendly blueoveralled owner. Annoyed, Julia elbowed her way into the conversation.

'Do you mind? I can handle this myself. Why don't you get my bags out of the car while you're waiting?' To her satisfaction she was obeyed with a shrug. He was obviously glad to get rid of her.

Julia arranged for a tow and a quote on repairing the car and then wondered what to do next. Craemar was about twenty kilometres away. Perhaps she could ring Richard and ask him to pick her up, she didn't want to ask any more favours of her erstwhile chauffeur.

An ear-shattering sound came from behind her as she stood on the forecourt pondering. She turned to see a huge Mack truck turning off the road and as it came closer she could see the driver, perched high up behind the wheel. It was a university friend of Ben's, John Seymour.

'Hi Julia, long time no see.' He grinned as she ran over to the cab of the truck. He cut the engine and leaned out of the open window. 'What are you doing in this god-forsaken spot?'

Julia explained and John made appropriate noises of sympathy. 'Why don't you come with me?' he suggested. 'I'm doing a delivery to Whitianga and picking up a new load tomorrow. I can do a slight detour and drop you off.'

'Could you? You won't get into trouble will you?' asked Julia anxiously. She knew how few and far between jobs for students were.

John gave her a wink. 'Perk of working for the family firm. You sling your stuff into the cab, there's plenty of room, I'll just go over and get some cigarettes and a snack.'

He jumped down from the truck and Julia gave him a hug of gratitude. She raced back to where the big man was standing with her bags.

'Thanks for the lift,' she panted. 'I've got another one from here.'

'Is that wise?' he asked drily.

'I don't see the difference between travelling with him and travelling with you,' Julia said tartly. He must have seen the hug and jumped to his own conclusions. It obviously hadn't even occurred to him that she might know the driver of the truck.

'I rest my case,' he said, but didn't try to read her a lecture. Non-involvement seemed to be his speciality.

'Thanks for the lift,' Julia called out after his retreating back and received a careless wave in acknowledgement. She battled to stow her two suitcases and handbag in the truck and climbed in after them to wait patiently for John.

The trip was fun. Julia liked being perched up above the rest of the lowly road-dwellers and John was a pleasant companion. He was intending to stay the night at Whitianga with his aunt and when he asked whether she'd like to have dinner with them Julia accepted with alacrity, thinking that Richard should still have a good deal left in his hamper.

'Let me report in first, though,' she said. She didn't want Richard to worry when she didn't arrive to cook his dinner!

Since the truck was too large to tackle Craemar's long, over-grown gravel driveway they had to park it on the roadside and leg it the rest of the way, carrying a bag each. When the house came into sight Julia paused for a moment, admiringly.

The colonial timber merchant who gave the house his name had done himself proud. He had begun its construction in the 1830s using imported red brick and native timber and as the two-storeyed edifice grew he had tacked on extra rooms to the design so that it had an oddly asymmetrical appearance by the time the last nail was hammered in five years later. Julia loved it for its oddness. It was a house with character, and most importantly of all, it had a fabulously large kitchen that was a joy to work in.

Julia lead John up the wide front steps to the white

marble portico, a fussy, twentieth-century addition, and
Julia pounded on the heavy kauri door with the ornate
brass knocker. Silence. For several minutes they
knocked and called without luck.

'Would you mind going around the side to have a
look in the garage—I'll go and open the kitchen door.'
Julia said, and they split up.

Richard could have gone out for the afternoon, Julia
supposed as she lifted the flowerpots surrounding the
back doorstep to find the one which hid the key. It was
there, just as Connie had told her, and Julia used it in
the stiff, old-fashioned lock and went into the silent
kitchen. Dusk was beginning to slip into darkness and
Julia switched on lights. The colours of the kitchen were
warm—browns and yellows with natural wood cupboards, but the room itself was very cold and empty,
not a dish out of place. No sign of Richard's hamper
either, not even in the pantry. A nasty suspicion
sneaking up on her, Julia turned as John came panting
up the stone steps.

'All locked up,' he said, pleasant round face creased
in puzzlement. 'There's even a cobweb on the lock so
I'd say he hasn't garaged his car while he's been here.'

'*If* he's been here,' said Julia grimly. 'I'll just go and
have a look in his room.'

It was upstairs, one of the rooms which opened out
on to the north-facing balcony, and it proved to be as
empty as the kitchen. It was spotless and there was a
fire set in the grate, but there were no clothes in the
wardrobe.

'The rat!' cried Julia as she swooped back into the
kitchen, to find John had fetched her bags from the
front of the house. 'He's not here!'

'Perhaps he changed his mind,' John offered.

'Oh no he didn't,' said Julia, seeing it all now. She
had been neatly manoeuvred into offering to make up
that hamper, which was probably even now being
consumed in some snug hideaway by Richard and his

latest dolly-bird. No wonder he had oozed charm when he had picked it up, his conscience had been pricking him. Not enough to confess, of course. Well, Richard Marlow, you'll get yours, Julia promised with silent wrath as she took her bags into the room which was to be hers. It was one of Henry Craemar's afterthoughts, bulging out from the side of the kitchen, the only bedroom on the ground floor. A box bed took up one end of the room, a mirrored bureau and huge old wardrobe the other. There was a small handbasin too, but if Julia wanted a bath she would have to troop upstairs to the main bathroom. She marched out again to John, determined that the discovery of Richard's little practical joke would not spoil her evening.

It was just after midnight when John drove her back to Craemar in his aunt's comfortable Wolsey. Refusing his offer to come in and check the dark house Julia dashed around to the kitchen door and fumbled for the key under the pot where she had replaced it. It wasn't there. Julia swore softly and pulled her jacket closer around her. It was freezing!

She circled back around to the front of the house and looked up. Ahhh! A window was slightly ajar, she could see the moonlight gilding the bottom of the white sash. Richard's room. He must have arrived while she was out and was now sound asleep, the deep sleep of the guilty!

Without a second thought Julia slipped over to the wooden fire-escape which was fixed to the corner of the house. Rapidly, silently, she climbed up and over the rail of the balcony. She quietly tried the french windows to Richard's room. Locked—she had expected that. Carefully she pushed the sash window far enough up so that she could squeeze through. Like a wraith she glided across the polished floorboards and paused beside the humped bedclothes, savouring her moment of revenge.

Taking a deep breath she reached out and ripped the bedclothes from the bed, letting out a shriek like a banshee as she did so:

'Ricky, Ricky, my idol!' she threw herself at the prone figure as it jerked to life, thrusting Richard back down on to the bed as she poured out her hysterical pleading. 'Darling, Ricky, let me be yours for one night of love.' She dug her fingernails deeply into the bare chest beneath her, feeling him wince with glee. 'Take me, take me, carve your name on my body ... it's already on my heart!' She tried to stifle her giggles with hot and heavy melodrama.

Julia wasn't quite sure when she realised something was wrong. By now Richard should be roaring with temper, or convulsed with laughter. And surely ... surely Richard didn't have all that hair on his chest ... her hand explored with sudden trepidation. My God— it wasn't Richard! Julia started to rear backwards off the bed when a dark shape snaked out from the bed and grabbed her wrist.

'Loath as I am to disappoint you, I am not "darling Ricky".'

Julia froze. That voice ... that pedantic phrasing—it couldn't be! The dark figure in the bed rose up ... and up, while Julia's heart sank in horrified disbelief. There was a click, and the bedside lamp sprang into yellow brightness.

The owner of the gunmetal grey Maserati regarded her frozen features with sleepy resignation.

'Why is it, I wonder, that I don't feel surprised to see you?'

CHAPTER THREE

'You!' Julia squeaked crassly. 'What are *you* doing here?' She wrenched her wrist out of his bear-like grip and leapt accusingly to her feet.

'What does it look like I'm doing?' His hand dropped in support as he heaved himself more upright in the bed, the feather duvet falling away to his waist. His shoulders and chest were massive under the black silk pyjamas, the thick mat of hair she had felt when she had thrown herself on to him revealed by the unbuttoned jacket. What a body! The thought came unbidden and Julia hurriedly qualified it—if you had a liking for all-in wrestlers.

'This is Richard's room,' Julia declared, taking a quick look around to confirm the fact.

'It also happens to be the only bedroom in the house with a fire made up,' came the pleasant reply. 'Speaking of which, would you mind shutting the window as you go out again, it's creating quite a draught.'

Julia twitched her shoulders straight and marched over to the window, hauling down the sash with a crash. Having made her point she went back to the bedside to demand of the bland, sleepy face: 'What have you done with Richard?'

It was a stupid thing to say. If he was a criminal psychopath who'd stuffed Richard up the chimney he wasn't likely to admit it. He could just as easily dispose of her with one swipe of a large paw. She ought to feel frightened, or at least apprehensive, but she didn't.

'I have done nothing with Richard. I have no idea where he is, and what is more I don't care. It's late and I would *like* to get some sleep.' His unusually soft voice was further husked by sleep and the grey hair stood up in little points where the movements of his head against the pillow had disturbed its straightness. He must be a restless sleeper, thought Julia, distracted for a moment. In the car his chin had been smooth, immaculately shaven, but now its contours were roughened by pepper and salt whiskers. The general air of ruffled untidiness made Julia soften towards him. She couldn't very well blame him for Richard's vagaries.

'May I suggest,' he continued, shattering the illusion of vulnerability, 'that you pass along your groupie-grapevine the gloomy news that the country's teenage heart-throb is not currently in residence.'

'Groupie-grapevine!' Julia's voice neared squeak-level again. 'I am *not* a groupie. I happen to be a friend . . .'

'That's what they all say,' he interrupted with precise distaste. 'I wonder how your old-fashioned parents would feel about *this* situation?'

His words reminded her of their manner of meeting.

'Are you a friend of the Marlows? If you'd said you were coming here you could have given me a lift all the way.'

'I didn't realise I was obliged to inform you of my travel plans,' he said, with mild sarcasm. 'Besides, I got the impression you preferred the company of the handsome young truck driver.'

'He was a friend too,' Julia told him, frowning at his sceptical look. 'And I happen to have known Richard for years.'

'So have several thousand other young women.'

'Does Mrs Marlow know you're here?' Julia firmly ignored the impulse to argue further. First she must find out who he was and why he was here. Had one of the family broken the rules already and invited a guest?

'No, but I assure you she would be unconcerned if she did know.'

Julia doubted it. Should she ring Connie in the morning and let her know? What if she wanted him to leave? What if he didn't want to go? Julia couldn't

imagine herself bodily ejecting him. Maybe Mrs
Brabbage could do that, since they were of a similar
size. Julia grinned at the upturned face but there was no
answering smile.

'Who are you?' she tried again. 'And how did you get
in?'

He hesitated before answering, then seemed to resign
himself to the fact that she was not budging without an
answer. 'With a key. Now would you mind . . .'

'The one from under the flowerpot!' That put him within the privileged circle. 'No wonder I couldn't find it.'

'You mean you do use conventional entrances on
occasion? How about using a conventional exit.' He
pointed to the door, the long silk-clad arm command-
ingly straight. He looked and sounded as if he was used
to being obeyed.

'At least tell me how long you intend staying,' she
pleaded. She was the one who would be looking after
him, even if he didn't know that yet. She looked
forward to disabusing him of the groupie notion,
though she couldn't blame him for it after her silly
behaviour in his car.

He leaned back on the double pillows with a sigh,
closing his eyes as he did so. The thick lashes threw tiny
half-circles of shadow on the hard planes of his cheeks.
The lamp light bleached the pale face of all expression
so that it looked as if it had been carved out of cold
white marble by the bold, sweeping strokes of a master
sculptor.

'I said . . .' Julia raised her voice, thinking he must be
drifting off.

The heavy lids lifted. 'Unfortunately, I heard what
you said. Your curiosity is ill-timed to say the least.
Can't this wait until daylight?'

'Don't you want to know what *I'm* doing here?' Julia
asked incredulously. Nobody could be that incurious.
Why, *she* could be a psychopathic murderess!

'I know what you're doing here,' he said. 'And I'm

even less impressed with your wisdom than I was this afternoon.'

'Well, I'm staying here too,' Julia offered gratuitously. 'I happen to be——'

'Resident groupie?' The full lower lip tightened with irony.

'I told you I'm not a groupie,' Julia insisted impatiently, against all the evidence. 'I'm the cook.'

The irony on his face intensified as he pushed himself up from the pillows. Julia stepped back involuntarily. It was like the raising of the Titanic. 'Why, Jean, you've lost a lot of weight since I saw you last,' he drawled.

'You know very well I'm not Mrs Brabbage,' Julia told him hastily. 'I'm taking her place for a while. Mr Brabbage has had an operation.'

'You're cook . . . in an empty house?'

'You're here.'

'Unexpectedly. So who were you planning to cook for, if you can cook at all?'

The professional slur annoyed Julia. 'I'm a qualified Cordon Bleu chef,' she snapped.

'Where did you qualify—the cradle?' he asked, quite reasonably, in the circumstances. 'What's the recipe for Eggs Benedict?'

'Wha . . . what?' The staccato question came out of the blue and Julia's brain jammed on all frequencies. This was too much on top of a troublesome afternoon and the wine she had imbibed freely at dinner, knowing she wasn't going to have to drive.

'It's . . . um . . . it's eggs. It's made with eggs,' she said lamely. She had prepared the damn dish a hundred times!

She was rescued by the snap of his fingers. 'J. Fry. Of course, you must be Janette, Mrs B's niece. I should have recognised you from her description! You'd better not let her find out that you haunt Richard's room in the early hours of the morning.'

Julia was gaping at him. Janette was legendary in the

Craemar annals. Having heard Mrs B on her favourite
subject Julia suspected that the not-so-innocent Janette
had had her dubious achievements embroidered to
make a symbolic point. She was everything that was
wrong with modern youth, according to Mrs B. It was
not flattering to be mistaken for an irresponsible,
promiscuous, high-school drop-out.

'My name is Julia, not Janette,' she declared hotly.
She didn't know the girl's last name and obviously
neither did he. He *had* remembered Julia's though.
'And you still haven't told me who *you* are.' She
hooked her thumbs through the loops of her jeans and
rocked aggressively on her heels.

'Inquisitive little thing, aren't you?' he said, not
believing a word of what she said, but giving in in the
hope it would get him some sleep. 'I'm Hugh.'

'Hugh who?' Julia asked blankly. It sounded
ridiculous but neither of them cracked a smile.

'Doesn't your intimate family knowledge run to the
less famous members of the family?'

Julia gasped at the outrageous implication. She could
only remember the G. B. H. part, but she was certain
that his surname had not been Marlow on that business
card. 'You liar!'

'How so?' he enquired, unperturbed. He couldn't
have expected to be believed.

'The Marlows have red hair . . .'

'Charles doesn't.'

'. . . and they're all built like bean-poles, not like . . .
like *tanks*.' Julia ignored his valid point. 'And you're
too old.'

'For what?' The grey ghost of a smile flitted behind
his eyes.

'To be Hugh,' Julia insisted. 'You must be at least
thirty-six.'

'Thirty-four,' he corrected drily.

'You look older,' she told him, too annoyed for
polite fiction. 'That would make Connie how old when

you were born . . .?' She did some mental arithmetic, one of her weak points. The silence lengthened.

'About fifteen,' he offered softly. 'However, I don't see that I'm under any obligation to explain the ramifications of my family tree to all and sundry. Good night.'

This time Julia didn't argue, she was feeling pretty tired herself. They could sort out the confusion in the morning. The stranger was already settling down under the duvet, reaching for the light as she closed the door behind her.

In a way it was reassuring to know that there was somebody else in the house, thought Julia as she guided herself down the moonlit stairs, especially someone large. He might be an unknown quantity, but in their two brief meetings she had gained the impression that he would be a rock in times of strife. To oppose him head-on would be to dash yourself to pieces. Much better to flow peaceably around him.

Her head had barely touched the pillow when she awoke to the sound of a clatter in the kitchen. It was barely light and the nip on her nose told her that there had been an overnight frost. She groaned as she heard another clatter. Don't tell me he's up already! She dragged herself up and scrambled into thick corduroy trousers and a polo-necked sweater with patch elbows. After dashing her face in lukewarm water at the basin and running a quick brush through her hair she strode into the kitchen, prepared to assert herself.

'Hullo, Julia. I'm sorry, did I wake you? I just brought in some of the supplies on that list you sent down. I went shopping in Whitianga on Friday but didn't have time to bring them over when I got back.'

'Time I was up, anyway, Mrs B,' said Julia, beaming at the large, ruddy-faced woman who stood in the centre of the kitchen.

'I thought I'd come along early and get going,' Jean Brabbage rolled up her sleeves, revealing beefy forearms, and continued merrily on, telling Julia about Jack's progress and how he liked to be left to himself in the mornings and cataloguing the work she intended to get through before the Marlows arrived. Jean was as talkative as she was big and Julia kept smiling and nodding, awaiting her chance.

'I was expecting Richard to be here already,' she managed, when the other woman paused for a fat breath.

'Huh!' A disapproving sniff. 'I got his room ready for him, even offered to come over and cook for him. But he rang and told me he was spending the weekend with a friend in Thames. A girl.' Another sniff, but before she could enlarge on her darkest suspicions, Julia nudged her back on to the right track.

'But someone's using his room.'

It was like flicking a light switch. The plump round face illuminated. '*He* would never be so ungracious. Let me know on Friday that he was coming down, and told me not to bother about him until today. Master Richard, now, he wouldn't dream of coping by himself for a weekend. Helpless he is.'

'But who is he?' cried Julia, nearly bursting with curiosity.

'Why, Mr Hugh, of course,' Jean Brabbage sounded horrified that anyone could not know who he was. 'I told him to take the room I had aired and made up.'

Julia sank into a chair beside the well-scrubbed kitchen table, now covered with Jean's bulging paper bags and cartons. He couldn't have been telling the truth!

'He's not Hugh *Marlow*?'

'Not Marlow, no,' came the baffling reply. 'He's Hugh Walton.'

Now she remembered G.B.H. Walton. 'I don't understand.'

'He's adopted,' came the bombshell reply. 'I was here when they first brought him home. Scrawny little thing

he was, only twelve, quiet as a mouse with those big
grey eyes and whispery voice.'

Scrawny! 'We are talking about the same person,
aren't we?' said Julia, as Jean rustled about the
shopping. 'I would have thought he's more of a lion
than a mouse.'

Jean chuckled. 'He is now. Half-starved he looked
then. And such an appetite; you'd have thought he had
never seen food before! Probably hadn't seen much,
come to that. He made up for it though, sprouted like a
beanstalk. Very fine athlete at school, could have been
Olympic class if he'd put it before his studying. Of
course all that bookwork's paying off now. He has his
own law firm, lectures at university, writes books ...
deserves every bit of it, I say. Be Prime Minister one
day I shouldn't wonder.'

What an accolade, thought Julia. Jean Brabbage
usually tempered every opinion with pessimism.

'It's strange, I never knew that the Marlows had
adopted a child. Nobody ever mentions it,' Julia angled
for a little more relevant information.

'Mr and Mrs Marlow aren't ones to broadcast their
private business, but it was never a secret,' Jean obliged.
'Mind you, it was all a long time ago and of course Mr
Hugh isn't in show business. He has a proper job.'

Julia choked back her laugh. Not even Richard at his
most persuasive and Michael at his most convincing
could persuade Jean that acting was work. Play-acting,
she called it, but was still proud of the famous family
she worked for.

'Did you tell him the family were coming down?' she
asked the million-dollar question.

'I thought he would know about that. Doesn't he?'
Julia shook her head. 'I thought it was funny, him
wanting to come down. Mr Hugh is a very reserved sort
of person.'

'Does he often come down by himself?' Julia thought
the reserve was probably stubbornness. Why was he so

anxious to avoid his family, he should be grateful that he had such a large and loving one? Actually, it wasn't so surprising that Connie and Michael should adopt, they were people of boundless affection and generous instincts.

'Not as often as he used to,' she sounded disappointed about it. 'He used to study down here while he was at law school. Didn't throw weekend-long parties with rowdy friends and brazen hussies, or spend most of his time drinking and carrying on like nobody's business.'

Julia didn't have much difficulty guessing the culprits. Richard and Steve had gone through the normal male metamorphosis, it seemed. But not Hugh, of course.

'The boys must have just been babies when he was adopted then,' she ventured, still on the trail of the enigma.

'They were only two. Mr Hugh was very good with them, for all he was quiet and withdrawn, and with the others, too, when they came. There was no jealousy and he never got nasty or tough with them. Very gentle, he was, not like most boys are.'

That soft voice still bespoke gentleness, yet of a detached kind that Julia misliked. The study of law required a tough and resilient mind, not a quiet, gentle personality. So which was he—Mrs B's darling or Richard's dry-as-dust lawyer who needed·reminding of his family obligations?

'How come he was adopted, what happened to his parents?' dared Julia, but this was too much, even for the garrulous Mrs B.

'I don't rightly know, they died I think,' she said, her face acquiring the faintly glazed look of an accomplished gossip forced to withhold a fascinating titbit. Julia respected her enormous self-restraint.

'What time does he have breakfast?' The big, wooden pendulum clock on the wall said seven and in Julia's mind the seed of an idea began to germinate. A cross between an apology and an explanation.

'He doesn't have any, at least only coffee and toast, and he likes to get that himself, so don't you worry. Now, I must get on and give his room a good clean. He's here to work on another book, you know.'

Julia knew that Hugh's room was the attic. She had never been up there but Connie had told her that it had been converted especially for her eldest son. It even had an *en suite* bathroom so that except for food he could be completely self-sufficient up there. The legal eagle's eyrie!

As Jean clumped heavily up the stairs Julia got busy. First she put all the purchases away, whipping around opening cupboards to check that everything was where she remembered it. She unpacked the tools of her trade and stepped into the cool, walk-in stone pantry and took out four smooth, brown farm eggs. She fetched a loaf of bread from the bread-bin and a few ham slices from the kitchen refrigerator.

She put the eggs on to poach and quickly toasted four rounds of bread, buttering them and laying on the ham slices. Jean must have lit the black coal-burning range when she came in, but Julia decided to use the electric one this morning. Although she loved cooking over flame, it always took her a few days to reaccustom herself to the element of risk involved.

While the eggs stayed warm in the oven she used Buster to make a quick Hollandaise sauce, hoping the ghastly row wouldn't annoy the man upstairs.

She had just placed the eggs on the rounds of toast and was pouring the sauce over the top when Jean reappeared to fetch the window-cleaner. Julia asked if she would mind taking Hugh's breakfast in, on her way upstairs.

'But I told you, he doesn't eat breakfast,' Jean regarded the beautifully set tray in dismay.

'He told me he likes Eggs Benedict,' fibbed Julia.

'And it can't hurt to offer. He won't be able to start work until you've finished.'

'I suppose not,' said Jean dubiously. 'Poached eggs is it?'

'Poached eggs,' agreed Julia with a grin. Good, plain cooking was Jean's forte; garnish was a foreign language.

Half an hour later, having eaten her own eggs, Julia was washing the dishes when the tray was returned.

'Good morning,' she carolled cheerfully to the man filling the doorway.

'Good morning,' he returned quietly, setting the tray down on the kitchen table. He had eaten everything, Julia noticed.

'Would you like some coffee now?' she turned to ask.

'No thank you.' He watched her hands drip soap suds on to the linoleum floor.

'I hope you didn't say anything too indiscreet to Mrs B.' Julia met his level stare.

'I'm never indiscreet.'

'How boring,' said Julia, believing it. 'I suppose you're now satisfied that I'm not the notorious Janette. Did you grill Mrs B under the bedside lamp?' What was it about him that urged her to tease. Perhaps because he reminded her of Phillip ... so correct, so thick-skinned.

'She sang your praises unasked. Thank you for the eggs, but they weren't necessary. I never eat breakfast.'

'Then you should.' Julia was genuinely concerned. 'Someone of your size especially. You need the fuel to last you through the morning, otherwise you're burning stored energy.'

'I have a slow metabolic rate,' Hugh Walton replied, so meekly that Julia frowned as she returned to her washing up.

'I mean it. Could you bring your tray over here so I can wash up your things?' As she took his plate she said, with a trace of smugness. 'You must admit now that I can cook.'

'I admit you can poach eggs,' he said in a neutral voice, and Julia laughed with delight.

'I was beginning to think you didn't have a sense of humour.' She could just imagine Mrs B's apologetic presentation, but he had known the eggs for what they were.

'That would be a fatal defect in my family,' he said gravely. 'But what makes you think I was joking?'

Julia looked at him uncertainly. Had she imagined the undercurrents to his remark? Could he really be totally without humour? 'Reserving judgment are you?' she asked, rubbing her nose with a soapy finger.

'Are you always afflicted with legalese, or is it especially for my benefit?'

'I can't help it,' Julia admitted. 'It just comes out. You're so ... so ...'

'Big?' he reminded her gently.

'Judge-like. I can see you in a wig and black gown putting on the black cap.'

Something shivered behind the impassive wall of his eyes, a fleeting pain that darted straight to Julia's tender heart. There were depths to the placid grey waters. No, not really like Phillip at all; she couldn't treat him with the slick superficiality she accorded her employer. Impelled by a vague and totally unfounded desire to distract him from whatever it was that had shadowed her flippant words, Julia added:

'I told you I wasn't a groupie, and I really am a friend of Richard's.'

'The one doesn't necessarily cancel out the other,' Hugh responded, raising his eyebrows as she clashed the dishes in the suds. 'Why don't you use the dishwasher?'

Julia broke out in a cold sweat at the very idea of the malevolent machine under the bench-top. 'I like doing dishes. Peaceful, mindless stuff.' She paused, and hurried on, 'Not to imply I haven't got a mind.' This was terrible, she was sounding more foolish with every word. 'I really am sorry about last night, disturbing you like that . . . it was only a joke. And as for the other, well, you can't really blame me. You don't *look* like a Marlow.'

'And you don't look like a Cordon Bleu chef,' he said, obviously having received a potted history from the voluble Jean.

'I know.' Julia sighed as she swished the last dish. 'It's the bane of my life. I'm twenty-four, you know.' It seemed important to stress her maturity to this oh-so-mature man.

'It would help if you acted it.'

Julia turned to him, hands on hips. 'I do; most of the time. But if you could have heard how patronising you sounded yesterday . . . I just couldn't be bothered to correct your false impression. Actually I thought you were going to blame my youth when you reported the accident.'

To his credit he looked surprised. 'I didn't report it, and I had no such intention.'

'I realise that now . . . but you can't trust anyone these days.' Her words rang hollow in the large kitchen. Somehow Julia felt that here *was* a man you could trust, to the ends of the earth if necessary. Not because of his size, or his profession, but because of his intrinsic integrity. Profound thoughts about a man she had only just met.

He kindly ignored the hackneyed phrase. 'Don't bother about breakfast for me in future, or lunch for that matter. When I'm working I like to grab something to eat at odd times. But I will come down for dinner.' This seemed to put a train of thought in action and he crossed the kitchen to the window which overlooked the shambles which was the vegetable garden.

'I heard about Jack Brabbage's hip, but I didn't think Connie would bother to employ a replacement cook—not until the summer, and by then Mrs B should be able to take over again. As it is there'll be precious little work for you to do.'

Julia resented his thinking she was on to an easy wicket, but what could she say that wouldn't blow the gaff on Richard? She applied herself diligently to wiping the cutlery, hoping he would keep his conclusions to himself.

'But she wouldn't do that, not Connie,' she heard him say with slow precision. 'She may be extravagant with words but she's thrifty with cash. A real housewife at heart. Why *are* you here?' No answer. 'Are you and Richard feathering a love-nest.'

'Of course not . . .' began Julia hotly and saw the satisfaction in his face as he sauntered back over, hands in the pockets of his grey woollen trousers, to confront her. It would have been better to pretend that she and Richard did have something going—after last night he wouldn't have found it hard to believe. 'Richard . . . we . . . I . . .' she stuttered, unable to utter the bare-faced lie.

'Is this one of his practical jokes?' The steely stare hardened. He knew his Richard.

'I'm only the cook . . .' she said weakly, hoping a dumb-blonde act might do the trick.

'Chef,' he corrected. 'And you're expecting to exercise your apparently considerable talents on someone.' His eyes narrowed thoughtfully and Julia weakened further. He only had to ask Mrs B and he would get the whole story in five minutes flat. What did she owe Richard? Nothing! He owed her. And it would serve him right if Hugh gave him a black eye for this particular episode. She wouldn't mind giving him one herself for putting her in this postiion.

'They're all coming,' she blurted. 'The whole family, for a month, because everyone's going to be tied up at Christmas.'

'And how long has this been arranged?'

'Connie hired me about a month ago.' Would he swear? Throw things about? Stamp upstairs and pack?

Of course not. 'Was it a general family conspiracy, do

you know? Or is it just Richard's delightful sense of humour?'

'Umm,' said Julia. Not wanting to throw her sometime friend completely to the wolf.

'Just Richard. Naturally. And no doubt he had planned to be here to break the gleeful news himself.'

'Umm,' said Julia again, and then thought that Richard deserved some defence. 'It wasn't entirely a joke. Richard thought it was about time that you were reminded that you were a member of a family . . .' she tailed off. He was looking down his long nose at her. There was a slight ridge half-way down its straightness, as if it had been broken once. He was very good at the quelling stare, Julia decided.

'I'm only too aware of my family.' The reply told her to mind her own business. 'And where do you fit into this brotherly gesture?'

'Nowhere,' she said hurriedly and tried her own version of the quelling stare. Baby blue eyes and a retroussé nose were not conducive to success, to the man before her she looked like a startled kitten. 'Richard just told me about the mix-up, and that Connie was having the decorators in so you wouldn't be able to go back *there* . . .' This time there was a definite wince. 'But I didn't know when you were coming and I certainly didn't cause you to crash into me.' Julia's mind skipped a groove, as it was wont to do. 'I think it was grossly unfair that you didn't mention at the time that you were a lawyer. It gave you an advantage.'

'I don't see how,' he countered calmly. 'You seem quite capable of standing up for yourself. You made certain that I was aware of my own culpability.'

While he, like a good lawyer, had admitted nothing. 'Yes, well, silence is provoking in a situation like that.'

'I get the feeling you're not difficult to provoke.'

Julia simmered down and laughed. 'That's a chef for you, we're volatile by nature. But I think it's only fair that you should say what's on your mind. Otherwise how can you expect people to understand your point of view? It's no good bottling it up and then getting mad when nobody takes any notice.'

'You're probably right,' Hugh Walton excused himself smoothly, 'but I must beg off any further philosophising. If I'm to get any work done I'll have to start before the horde descends.'

'You're going to *stay*!' Julia stared at his calmness.

'I don't seem to have much choice.' That was a lie. He was the kind of man who provides his own choices.

'B-but, Richard said you'd . . .'

'I can imagine. But Richard is prone to exaggeration. My attic is very private. It only has one door and entry is by invitation, as my family well knows. I shall survive a few hours of their company each day. I may even thrive on it, who knows?'

Julia certainly didn't. Was he being sarcastic? How stiff he sounded, standing there, coolly disposing of the family that had adopted him. Had he been too old when he came to them, to be influenced by his adoptive parents' enthusiasm for life? What had made him so mountainously placid? It had to be unhealthy—everyone needed outlets for their human emotions. She shivered. Perhaps it was just as well; in a rage Hugh Walton would be magnificently terrifying. But what of the softer passions?

'When is everybody due?' he asked, turning at the door.

'Any day now,' said Julia, unable to resist a probe: 'Aren't you even the *teeniest* bit annoyed?'

'I'm furious,' he said, with a calm sincerity that spoke volumes. 'But since there's nothing I can do . . .' He spread his large palms. From across the room Julia could see the fascinating life and head-lines deeply etched into the pale skin.

'Why don't you scream?' she asked. 'It might make you feel better.'

'I'd rather work, it's much more productive.'

Julia stared after him thoughtfully. Work. Is that where all his vitality went? Was there nothing left over for himself? Everything about him seemed grey and dull. Yet, she reminded herself, an uncut diamond was dull to the eye . . . all its beauty and fire locked inside, waiting to be released by the skilled hands of a craftsman. Julia was no diamond-cutter, but she *was* interested in people, and this man intrigued her by his very blandness. What was he like underneath? What made him the way he was? What thoughts and feelings did he conceal behind that poker face? Would she ever learn to read it?

I'll work you out, G. B. H. Walton, before I leave, she vowed silently. I might even get you to smile at me. That would be an achievement indeed!

CHAPTER FOUR

JULIA'S first week at Craemar was chaotic, but by the middle of the second she had established a satisfactory routine, and was beginning to enjoy herself.

Fortunately she had got her VW back within a few days, and the bill had not been severe, although the garage man had tsk-tsked over the car's general condition. As she lit the range on a freezing Thursday morning, pumping energetically on the bellows until the flames began to roar, Julia decided that she wouldn't report the accident to the insurance company after all. It wasn't worth it, since she would lose the excess on her policy, which was more than the price of the repairs. She'd have to discuss it with Hugh, though, *if* she got the chance. He was sticking rigidly to his word, appearing at dinner only and Julia couldn't help worrying over his eating habits. She could only guess that he had squirrelled away some provisions up there.

Kidneys in cream sauce and soft scrambled eggs: Julia skidded around the kitchen in her thick yellow socks, dancing to keep warm and singing along with the radio.

Michael Marlow seemed to be the only other one up. He had already been in for a cup of Julia's special Mexican coffee, and a chat, and was now at work in the downstairs study. He was a real darling. Thin, blue-eyed and fine-featured, he had a beautiful creamy voice that could rise to a parade-ground bawl when he lost his temper. Fortunately no one took his temper seriously, since it followed closely the progress of his play.

Richard, of course, had been the first arrival at the house, slinking in the kitchen door and throwing himself on Julia's mercy with a mumbled story about a long-lost school chum whom he had dropped in to see and couldn't, just *couldn't*, turn down the offer of a weekend's reminiscence. Julia didn't even ask what gender the 'chum' was. She must have made him feel doubly guilty, for now Richard was keeping her almost constant company, dogging her footsteps in the kitchen and generally making a nuisance of himself.

Watching Hugh take the wind out of his brother's sails had been reward enough. Richard was completely baffled and disgusted by the pleasant welcome Hugh gave each arriving member of the family. Not even his most outrageous baiting disturbed Hugh's calm and for days Julia was nagged about it.

'He must have said *something*, darling. He can't have swallowed it without a comment or two. If only I'd been *here*.'

Remembering why he hadn't, Julia had enjoyed putting on her dumb-blonde act and watching him gnash his teeth.

It was lovely to see everyone again. Olivia and Rosalind were as irrepressible as ever, short-cropped Olivia the slightly more serious of the two. Charley, topping Julia by almost a foot, voice long broken, was beginning to shrug off his former shyness and emerge as a person in his own right.

Only Steve struck a sour note. Listless, sullen and uncommunicative, he was obviously wrestling with a personal problem, determinedly rejecting all family overtures. Only with Julia did he seem to relax fractionally, possibly because she made no demands on him, held no expectations. He kept out of the way during the day, but often, later at night, he would sit at the bare, scrubbed table in the kitchen and watch Julia prepare the food for the next day. She didn't question him, but rambled on in her own, cheerful fashion during his long silences and listened curiously to his equally long, erratic, oddly detached monologues about pollution, nuclear warships and other blights on modern civilisation. He didn't pick at the food, as Richard did, just drank glass after glass of water. More often than not he was still there, staring into his glass, when Julia went off to bed. She longed to help in some way, but knew that pressure from her was the last thing he needed at the moment.

Breakfast was the one meal of the day that Julia liked to eat alone, in peace, and she was finishing off a left-over portion of kidney, dreamily gazing out of the window at the delicate wreaths of morning mist that lingered in the encircling bush, when her reveries were rudely interrupted.

It was Hugh, with a brusque request for morning tea to be served in the courtyard by the small swimming pool. A colleague, on her way back to Auckland from Tauranga, was stopping by to pick up part of Hugh's manuscript.

Some detour! 'Who is she?' popped out before Julia could stop it.

On the point of leaving Hugh raised a thick eyebrow. 'Does it make a difference?'

'If she's Indian or Chinese I might whip up something ethnic,' said Julia, cunningly, widening her eyes innocently.

'Her name is Ann Farrow. She's of English extraction. She's a senior lecturer in the Department of Computer Sciences at the University. Is that sufficient background for you to produce a simple tea and biscuits?'

'Married or single?' she shot back, encouraged by his sarcasm. Sarcasm was humour, wasn't it?

His mouth thinned and for a moment she thought he was going to say something rude. 'Single. She'll be arriving about eleven.'

Julia grinned as he stalked out. A computer expert, just his cup of tea! They probably didn't make love, just indulged in a bit of mutual programming. Julia's mind drifted into the realms of fantasy. What would Hugh be like in bed? Surely he would shed some of that self-restraint along with his clothes? Or perhaps, because of his largeness, he needed it even more. It must be a little like making love with a steam-roller! Julia giggled as she put her plate in the sink. Her thoughts roamed from fantasy to indecency as she tried to imagine Hugh in the flesh. She had never seen a naked man in reality, but basic knowledge of human biology filled the gaps. He had a magnificent chest, wide and hard and warmly furred, would the rest of him match up? Weren't feet and hands supposed to indicate the size of a man's vital parts? Julia blushed at the involuntary tingling sensation that invaded her as she remembered the large, capable hands on the Maserati's wheel.

Natural curiosity prompted her to mention the expected guest to Connie when she brought through the breakfast trolly.

'Oh Ann. I might have known she'd find an excuse to drop in while Hugh's here.'

'Is she nice?'

Connie wrinkled her face. 'A paragon. Brunette, cool, cerebral . . . just Hugh's type. To tell the truth I think she's a bit of a bore. And I think Hugh knows, at least I hope he does, that his chief attractions for Ann are his wallet and his status. She's convenient for him, though, and available.'

How terrible, thought Julia, to be accepted on the basis of yur convenience and availability. Was that *all* Hugh asked of a woman?

Baking for Hugh's guest suddenly gave Julia the idea for the perfect revenge on that wretch, Richard. She'd bake him a cake. A gorgeous, mouth-watering, tempting chocolate cake, made with loving care from the most revolting ingredients possible. She had seen it done before, as part of a secret prank on the part of fellow Cordon Bleu students, the day before a cooking contest.

It turned out perfectly; Julia crowed with delight
when she eventually took the innocuous-looking cake
from the oven. To disguise the odd smell—a mixture of
curry, mustard and pickles—she carefully covered the
entire surface with chocolate icing, liberally laced with
brandy. Finally she decorated the top with stiffly salted
cream and half-hid the cake on one of the back shelves
in the pantry. Richard was a confirmed pantry-raider, a
midnight-feaster extraordinaire; he wouldn't be able to
resist taking a piece, a big piece, Julia hoped cruelly.

Not long after she had baited her trap, Julia met up
with Richard in the hall and found herself breezily
accepting one of his silly dares. Her elation faded a little
when she found herself gingerly mounting the banister
rail at the top of the stairs and gulping as she looked
down the long, slippery slide.

'Come on scaredy-cat,' taunted Richard, safely at the
bottom. 'I've done it hundreds of times. Five dollars
you won't, and as a concession I'll stand here and catch
you as you come off.'

'Scaredy-cat' did it. Julia shoved off. It was much
steeper, and faster, than it had looked and Julia
scrunched her eyes shut. She screamed as she whizzed
around the tight corner at the landing, thighs
desperately gripping for balance, her red woollen skirt
billowing up around her legs. Richard stepped back a
pace as she shot at high speed towards him and she
shrieked curses at him: 'Richard, you swine, get back
th—ooophh!'

She hit him square in the chest with an almighty
thump and they both went sprawling on the hall mat in
a tangle of limbs. They lay there breathless for several
moments, trying to figure out who belonged to what.
Julia squirmed backwards and came up against
something rigid and uncomfortable. She moved her
head see what it was. Her gaze travelled up a grey-
trousered leg. . . . Oh no! She buried her face in the
nearest convenient spot—Richard's neck.

'I don't need to introduce Richard to you, Ann, but the lady in red underneath him is our ... cook. Ann Farrow—Julia Fry.' He stepped over them and carried on down the hallway. The only glimpse Julia got of his companion was a beautifully turned ankle atop a green stiletto heel. Richard was convulsing with laughter.

'It's all right for you,' Julia groaned. 'This sort of idiot thing is expected of you.'

'Only Hugh could carry off an introduction like that!' Richard gasped, then his laughter faded as he looked down at Julia's small face. 'But since we're here ... why don't we ...' He bent his head, kissing her full on the mouth.

'Don't, Richard ...' Julia pushed at him, annoyed not only by the inappropriateness of the moment, but also by the intensely love-like glint in the green eyes.

'Why not?' His hands slid around her waist, holding her still.

"Then Julia let me wooe thee,
Thus, thus to come unto me:
And when I shall meet
Thy silv'ry feet,
My soule Ile pour into thee."

On the last breath he kissed her again, a fervent, persuasive kiss that bewildered her. What on earth was he up to?

'When you've *quite* finished, Julia.' She wrenched her head frantically to one side to see Hugh leaning around the lounge door, frowning distastefully down at them. 'The tea?' he reminded her heavily. 'And Richard, there are less public, more comfortable places to do what you two seem to be intent on doing.'

Richard—the swine—laughed: 'When we get to your great age, big brother, we'll probably think the same. But when you're young and hot-blooded, anywhere, anytime will do, eh Julia?'

Julia was too busy struggling to her feet to answer,

horrified to discover that her skirt had been wrapped around her waist. She fled in disarray to the kitchen, frowning as she put on the kettle and began to lay up a tray. Why should she care what Hugh thought of her? He was already convinced that she was a flighty little piece, and she hadn't missed that pointed introduction . . . cook indeed! Obviously Hugh considered that a *chef* must have dignity, a chef must not roll about on the floor showing off black lace panties to all and sundry. She bit her lip. She was beginning to think that her jinx had extended itself from things mechanical to things Hugh. Always having been popular, and confident of being liked, it was unsettling to come up against someone who didn't respond to her sunny, open nature. And it was more than just the challenge of getting him to see her in a favourable light that gnawed at her, she genuinely wanted him to like her, to respect her as a person. She wasn't quite sure why, after all, she hardly knew the man, but he had succeeded in intriguing her and she was rather piqued that the interest wasn't returned.

Strolling thoughtfully out into the garden to look for surviving winter roses for the tea tray, Julia heard a loud clatter as she passed the lean-to behind the garden shed. Curious, she pushed back the old piece of sacking that hung down over the entrance.

'Charley!' She ducked into the gloomy interior. 'So this is where you disappear to every morning? What are you doing?'

Charley wiped his nose with a greasy hand and shrugged.

'Just mucking about.'

'What with?' On closer inspection the pieces of metal seemed to be arrayed in some kind of order. 'Are you making something?'

'A motorbike,' he blurted out, and then glared as though he expected her to laugh.

'Really!' There was no danger of laughter from Julia and her genuine awe had Charley's stubborn, square jaw relaxing. 'That's fantastic! Can you actually do it? How far have you got?'

'Well, I only found this stuff last Friday,' he replied with careful casualness which dissipated as he launched into a description of the difficulties involved in putting together the rusting parts he had discovered in the clutter of the big garage out front (which seemed to have been tacitly reserved for the grey Maserati). 'Course, I haven't got all the parts I need, but I have a pal whose Dad runs a garage. He lets me help with the cars sometimes when I stay. I've learnt an awful lot with him. Mr Franklin says I have a feel for engines.'

'Does he live in Taupo?' guessed Julia, thinking of Connie's Christmas woes.

'Why yes, how did you know? Anyhow, he says I should try for an apprenticeship, but ...' His enthusiasm abruptly tailed off, 'I dunno yet what I want to be.'

But of course he did. It was in his eyes, his flushed, earnest face when he talked about cars. She gave him a sympathetic smile, realising that he knew of Connie's hopes for his future.

'Since you're such a clever mechanic, maybe you should take a look at my car. It needs an overhaul, I'm told but I wouldn't know a spark-plug from a ... a ... motor arm.'

'Rotor arm,' corrected Charley with a touch of male superiority, and, eagerly, 'Would you really trust me?'

Julia had been half-teasing but she thought—why not? He was keen, and sensible enough to admit it if he couldn't cope.

'A man with a feel for engines?' She grinned cheerfully. 'Of course I would.'

'You ...' Charley inspected a grimy thumb-nail, 'you won't tell about it will you? I don't know that Mum would like me messing around out here.'

'If you do decide to be a mechanic, she's going to have to find out about it sometime,' said Julia gently.

'But not yet.' Boy became adult before her eyes. 'She's a bit worried about Steve at the moment; Dad too. There'll probably be a fuss ... I'd rather wait. I have to stay and sit School Certificate this year anyway.' Showing he had thought about it—probably, being Charley, long and hard and realistically.

'That sounds sensible,' agreed Julia, 'I ... oh my God!' Her shout made Charley jump. 'I left the kettle on. Hugh's tea!'

She streaked up to the house, taking the shortcut through the bushes at the side, intending to slip in through the french doors of the dining room. She stopped dead when she came in sight of the pool. There was Hugh, setting down the tray on a wrought iron table. Horrors! He must have had to make the tea himself.

It was too late to duck back the way she came so Julia tried to stroll nonchalantly past the couple at the table. She could see what Connie meant about Ann Farrow. Elegant to her blood-red fingertips. Supercilious too, thought Julia, with instant dislike.

'I see you found the tray,' brazened Julia as she drew level with Hugh's stony stare.

'You have leaves in your hair,' she was informed coolly and the woman smiled faintly, pityingly, at Julia's rather tousled appearance. No doubt they thought she and Richard had retired to the shrubbery.

'I was looking for some flowers, to put on your tray,' she explained to Hugh's polite scepticism.

'I would have preferred less decoration and more substance,' he said crushingly and Julia got another pitying glance. Goodness, the woman didn't think that she had set her cap at Hugh, did she? The bubble of laughter in Julia's throat deflated with a nasty gulp as she noticed the cake in pride of place on the tray.

'Where did you get that?' she squawked and, rapidly recovering, 'Actually I made that cake for tomorrow. I've some lovely biscuits for this morning.'

'The cake is fine, thank you.' Grey eyes were

unimpressed by her brilliant smile. 'You can bake another one for tomorrow. That *is* your job isn't it?' Not seducing male members of the household on the hall floor. The unspoken hovered in the air.

'The biscuits really are scrumptious, and there are some lovely scones too,' she wheedled. 'Why don't I just—ouch!' Her reaching hand received a smart rap across the knuckles.

'Julia.' The normally soft voice flattened out threateningly. 'We are having our tea. Would you stop hovering and go back to the kitchen? The cake stays.'

Julia sucked her knuckles in an agony of indecision. Should she, or shouldn't she tell him? One look at Hugh's grimly harassed face persuaded her to favour cowardice. Her legs automatically set themselves in motion while her normally fertile brain failed her. Several metres on she looked back. Hugh was cutting the cake, that beautiful chocolate monstrosity! She groaned and looked wildly around for a hiding place. The pool!

Two swift steps, a leap and a nicely timed scream that became real as she hit the water. It was freezing! Icy water rushed into her heavy clothes, dragging her down. It filled her nose and mouth and she kicked frantically for the surface.

'Help!' Her cry sounded satisfyingly shocked and weak and she let herself go under again, glad her body seemed to be going numb. She came up and floundered by the side of the pool, relieved to see that Hugh had abandoned the cake in favour of rescue.

'Take my hand,' he ordered, reaching down and engulfing her frozen fingers in a fiery grip. The muscles in his arm bunched thickly under the sleeve of his blue suit as he began to pull, but as she reached her other hand up to grab him Julia saw Ann Farrow out of the corner of her eye. She was about to bite into a large piece of cake. Selfish bitch, thought Julia incredulously, I might be drowning for all she cares!

She could never afterwards decide whether her next action was accidental or not. She jerked hard on Hugh's arm and, taken by surprise, he teetered on the edge— one more tiny little tug and . .

He toppled as if in slow motion, sending up an enormous splash as he hit the water. He came up quickly, his face only inches from Julia's, a picture of outrage.

'What in the devil did you think you were doing?' he demanded rigidly, through his teeth.

'I'm t-t-terribly sorry,' shivered Julia, her own teeth chattering quite violently. 'I think I slipped.'

At least she had taken Ann Farrow's mind off her stomach. She was there beside Hugh exclaiming with over-done sympathy as he heaved himself out of the water. Julia floundered out alongside, like a sprat beaching with a whale.

'Hugh, I——' she was stopped by the raising of a large, dripping hand.

'I think you've said, and done, quite enough, Julia. Save your explanations for another time.' He was shivering only a little, his immaculate suit soggily twisted, whereas Julia was vibrating like a tuning fork, her clothes plastered against the voluptuous curves of her body. On Julia, bedraggled looked sexy and the wind chill factor from Ann Farrow's direction increased markedly.

'Go and get dry,' Hugh instructed, beginning to peel off his wrinkled jacket.

'But——' A strangled sound from the wet monolith in front of her made obedience advisable, so Julia backed apologetically away, making a darting detour to scoop up the cake under cover of Ann Farrow's renewed expressions of concern. Julia doubted that they'd be thinking about tea for a while . . .

At dinner that night Hugh seemed his usual distant, cynical self over sweetbread vol-au-vents and buttery, herb-flecked roast chicken. Julia's hopes rose. Perhaps he was willing to forgive and forget.

Unfortunately Richard, who had taken Olivia in to Whitianga for the day, chose that moment to thrust a large and shiny spanner into the quietly meshing works.

'What on earth were you doing by the pool this morning, Julia?' he asked, helping himself greedily to niçoise salad and sweet, hot, caramalised shallots. 'We were just leaving when I saw you take a flying dive into the water. You weren't even wearing your togs.'

All eyes focused on Julia as she gibbered through a mouthful of winter lettuce. 'I ... I ... er, I lost my balance.'

'No you didn't,' insisted Richard. 'I saw you in my mirror. You jumped.' He grinned wickedly; he knew, he just *knew* he was getting her into trouble. Sure enough:

'You jumped?' Hugh enunciated in slow, silky tones, that wound their way threateningly around the table. 'Do you mean to tell me that you didn't fall—you jumped!'

Julia studied the chicken bones on her plate for the answer to the mysteries of the universe. There was a thick silence at the table. Even Steve was looking at her with riveted attention, instead of his usual restless, darting manner. Taking a deep, steadying breath Julia raised her eyes to Hugh. His black pupils had narrowed to pinpoints surrounded by hoar frost. His face was in rigid stillness, pale except for the very tips of his neat ears, which were slightly flushed. Not from embarrassment, Julia realised, her heart pounding.

'I ... I ...' She desperately wanted to soften that frigid stare.

'Don't bother to deny it.' The silk abruptly ripped to reveal the yawning steel trap beneath. 'It's written all over your guilty face. Perhaps you would care to enlighten me—us—as to your motives.'

'I ... it was a joke,' she began weakly, into the awed silence, intending to make a clean breast of the whole episode.

'A joke!' He sounded utterly contemptuous, for

which she couldn't blame him. He cut across her attempt to explain. 'And was it a joke that you hauled me in there with you?' There was a stifled gasp from more than one at the table. 'You embarrass me in front of a valued colleague *for a joke*? And do you intend to pay for the four hundred dollar suit you ruined ... or don't you find that quite so funny?'

Julia felt weighted to her chair by the force of his anger, all the more oppressive because it was so tightly contained.

'That part was an accident,' she mumbled, her anxious tongue tying itself up in knots. There was a lump in her throat and to her horror she felt close to tears. 'You see, I ...'

Crash! She, and everyone else, leapt as Hugh's hand came smashing down on the table top. Dishes rattled, the chandelier above their heads trembled.

'Don't lie! And you can take that innocent look off your face—it never did impress me very much. How in the hell did you get your qualifications, let alone practise them? I cannot imagine how anyone with a modicum of sanity ...' here he threw a caustic look at his mother, who merely blinked at this new, electrifying Hugh '... could trust you in a position of responsibility. If you're not careering dangerously around the countryside, or leaping uninvited into strangers' beds, you're indulging your infantile sense of humour—and you can stop snickering, Richard, because you're just as bad.' He returned to the attack, seemingly unconscious of the effect of his startling revelations on everyone else. 'Yesterday it was climbing trees and playing Tarzan—yes, Julia, I could see you perfectly well from my window—today it's pushing people into pools. What'll it be tomorrow—a little bit of arson for fun!'

Julia's urge to cry abruptly left her. Tarzan had been Richard's idea and Charley and Ros had been there too. It had all been good, clean fun. Hugh might have a right to be annoyed, but not to harangue her in public with all sorts of irrelevancies.

'At least I know how to laugh,' she retorted stiffly. 'You may not approve of my sense of humour but, thank goodness, not everyone is as stuffy as you. I'm sorry about the pool,' her annoyance making it sound as if she wasn't, '... but I intended to come and explain ...'

'Your intentions and your actions are sadly at variance. Are you sure this is the kind of job that suits you? You'd be better employed catering for a three-ring circus if you find slapstick so amusing!'

Shades of Phillip! 'It's better than not finding anything amusing at all!' cried Julia hotly, feeling she may as well be hung for a sheep as a lamb. 'And I'll thank you to remember that you're not my employer, Connie is, and she's quite happy to trust me.' Hugh's soft, derisive grunt infuriated her. 'What's so great about your oh-so-sane approach to life anyway? Does it make the world a better place to be? No it doesn't, it only makes it a little grimmer. The stuffed shirts of this world have made a damn fine mess of things as far as I can see. It's people like you who rationalise atomic bombs and pollute the earth with new scientific wonders. It's people like you who make life a chore instead of a joy.' She paused for breath, feeling that she was getting off the track. 'And I'll pay for your Goddamned suit when you pay for smashing into my car!'

Michael Marlow murmured something disbelieving, but no one was interested.

'You are not a member of this family, Julia Fry, however much you might *try*,' said Hugh, with slow, crackling cruelty. 'As you so charmingly pointed out you are Connie's employee. Please act like it.' Pushing away his half-eaten meal Hugh rose to his feet, his voice reverting to its habitual softness as he struck the Parthian blow. 'When you're a little less hysterical, I'll listen to your apology.'

He slammed the door as he went, and the chandelier

shimmered again. Julia could see the questions forming a thicket in the air. 'I'm sorry, excuse me, will you?'

She escaped to the empty kitchen, stomach churning. She hated arguments. Worse, Hugh had been right, there was no excuse for hurling insults at her employer's son over the dinner table. Now Connie might feel obliged to fire her. Oh, why had she lost her temper! Better to have burst into tears, at least she might have gained a bit of sympathy that way. And now Hugh's opinion of her was worse than ever! For the first time she considered the possibility that she *was* irresponsible. She was far too prone to jumping impulsively into situations without properly considering the consequences. Accepting Richard's dare, for one thing ... and childishly baking him that disastrous cake. They weren't the actions of a mature, thinking adult. Perhaps she should try and curb some of her natural high spirits, exercise a bit more self-control. At least her humour and optimism ensured that her tempers never lasted very long, but Hugh was a different kettle of fish. These strong, silent types were apt to brood. He might smoke and smoulder away in that attic of his for years ... she *had* better apologise.

She was still trying to psyche herself up to it half an hour later when Connie sought her out.

'I'm sorry, Connie, I should never have said what I did,' began Julia, gloomily rattling the coffee cups.

'We don't condone censorship in this house, literary or verbal,' responded Connie easily. 'Hugh can be infuriating, I know, but perhaps in this case your temper did get the upper hand. What was it all about?'

Julia explained, and Connie dutifully kept a straight face until it came to the cake, and the pool.

'Oh Julia, couldn't you have done something less ... dramatic,' her voice trembled. 'Pretended to faint or something.'

Julia looked at her, her mouth falling open. So simple a ploy hadn't occurred to her fevered brain. 'Well ... I, er . . . I'm no actress, Connie, I probably wouldn't have been able to carry it off. Anyway, I don't think the *valued colleague* would have been diverted by anything less than my untimely death.'

'Forget Ann, that was only Hugh rubbing it in by being pompous, he's good at it isn't he?' The jewel-bright eyes narrowed thoughtfully. 'I've never seen Hugh quite so . . . annoyed, at least not for a very long time. He usually reserves his arguments for obscure points of law and lets everyday nuisances go hang—like Richard keeping it secret that we were coming . . . I heard about that. Hugh is very good at ignoring what he doesn't like, he can be aggravatingly single-minded about it. He should be case-hardened now, having put up with our antics for so long. Bawling you out was . . . why it was positively *Marlowish*.' She paused. 'I wonder whether that's occurred to him yet?'

'I suppose I'll have to go up and apologise,' Julia prodded, anxious for some biased advice.

'I suppose you'd better,' agreed Connie quietly. 'It would clear the air.' She settled herself down at the kitchen table. 'Actually the reason I trotted in was to tell you something that might help you in your dealings with Hugh. I know he's a difficult man to approach on a personal basis, but please don't think that because he doesn't laugh easily it's because he's a cold and humourless man. He's not. But he finds it awkward to cope with emotionalism. It's the boyish part of a man that likes to laugh and play the fool, but Hugh has nothing of the boy left in him. He doesn't have the memories of innocent joy that most of us acquire in childhood. You knew he was adopted, of course? Well, the circumstances in which he came to us were . . . very sad; he was very withdrawn and very mistrustful of people. We loved him and gave him security, but we couldn't obliterate the past for him.

'So please, don't judge him too harshly, Julia. He is extremely self-aware, overly so, and is very conscious of a lack in himself. Coming face to face with someone as happy and easy-going as you, must only throw his deficiencies into relief.'

'Oh God, I couldn't have said anything better planned to hurt him, could I?' Julia buried her head in her hands, reliving every bitter word she had uttered, cursing her runaway tongue. What right had she had to criticise Hugh when she was such a bitch herself? It didn't help to know that Connie's hesitant 'very sad' had glossed over a great deal of obviously painful detail. Julia longed to ask questions, but her innate sensitivity held her back. Connie had made concession enough telling her this much. It was really none of Julia's business and she knew that Hugh would hate to be discussed in such a way. She understood him better now, but only a little, and she wanted badly to make everything right between them. Yet she mustn't let him see any sympathy, his pride would revolt at the very thought, and he would be suspicious if she suddenly grovelled. If only she wasn't so confused about her feelings ... her original dislike all jumbled up with compassion and curiosity, and despair that he seemed to have so little of her beloved laughter in his life.

'I didn't mean to heap coals of fire,' Connie hastened to console her. 'Hugh has a pretty thick skin, and a lot of what you said was true ... that's probably what riled him. Hugh likes to think of himself as impenetrably private. It must be shattering to find a slip of blonde reading him like a popular paperback.'

Julia gave a small, weak smile. 'I'm afraid at this stage I'm only just following the pictures. Thanks, Connie.'

'Off you go and get it over with, I'll make coffee. He'll be heartily regretting his bearishness by now, you should get a fair hearing. Go on—shoo!'

Exit stage left. Julia obeyed the director's command.

CHAPTER FIVE

THE faint spittering sound impinged again on Julia's semi-consciousness. She groaned and sat up, squinting at the luminous dial of her watch. Six o'clock. The spitter became a rattle and Julia reluctantly knelt up, shivering in her candy-striped nightshirt, and thrust open the window above her box bed.

Richard, looking disgustingly energetic, let fall a handful of gravel and threw his arms wide in the wintery gloom.

> "Get up, get up for shame, the Blooming Morne
> Upon her wings presents the god unshorne.
> See how Aurora throwes her faire
> Fresh-quilted colours through the aire:
> Get up, sweet slug-a-bed and see
> The Dew-bespangled Herbe and Tree."

'Get lost!' Julia heaved one of her embroidered cushions at him and he fielded it with a grin.

'What a grouch you are of a morning, sweeting.'

'Do you know what time it is?' Julia demanded. 'I don't have to get up for another hour. What on earth are you doing?'

Richard executed a few shuffling dance steps. 'Appreciating the gift of life. Walking . . . thinking. Why don't you come out and welcome in the dawn with me?'

Julia eyed him suspiciously. Richard was a night-owl, all his energies diverted into his performance. The rest of the time he conserved his strength with sloth-like skill.

'No thank you.' She shivered even more as the cold air crept inside her neckline. 'What did you wake me up for?'

71

'Connie and Michael are going down to Hahei today, did Connie tell you? Visiting some great aunt or other. How about a picnic lunch for us at Cook's Beach?'

'Do you think the weather will hold?' It had been heavily overcast the day before.

'Too cold for rain . . . there's a frost out here you know, sweet slug-a-bed.'

'OK,' Julia yawned and stretched mightily, it would be nice to have a day away from the house.

'Great. I knew you wouldn't let me down. We'll have a gorgeous time, I promise.' He now seemed eager to get away.

'Well, hey!' Julia called after him as he walked away. 'Will you tell the others, or shall I?'

'What others, sweet Juliet?' Richard began to whistle as he disappeared around the side of the house.

'Damn!' Julia slammed the window shut, annoyed at having walked straight into his trap. He knew that she had been trying to avoid being alone with him lately. His attempts to fan a romance between them were becoming a real pain, and she had no doubt that he had more of the same on his agenda for today.

Well, two can play at that game, fella, Julia smiled wickedly to herself as she snuggled down for a few more minutes in her warm nest. After facing up to Hugh as she had last night, she felt able to cope with anything.

It had taken a determined courage to mount those narrow attic stairs and confront the eagle in his eyrie, or on the edge of his eyrie—for Hugh had refused to allow her inside. He had opened the door and stood, squarely blocking the rectangle of light, arms crossed over his massive chest.

'Er . . . can I come in?' she had asked meekly, trying to decipher the unreadable expression on his face.

'No.'

Her courage dwindled even further. So much for him regretting his bearishness. In fact she preferred the bear to the great stone face before her now.

'Please . . . I came to . . . I want to . . .'

'I know why you came, Julia, why don't you just get on with it?'

Julia swallowed. 'You're not making this easy for me.'

'Is there some reason I should?'

Julia struggled with uncertain emotions. It was difficult to retain your sympathy with a man who could be so effectively nasty with so little effort. But what struck even deeper into her tender heart was the realisation that such nastiness was really only a form of defence. He was a man slow to trust, and he certainly had no reason to trust Julia with the merest glimpse into his private life. That was guarded, as was his room, by sheer force of will. Julia hated hurting others, and never before had she pushed herself where she wasn't wanted, but something about Hugh roused an instinct in her, at once aggressive and protective, a curiosity that constantly craved appeasement.

'Look, can't we go in and sit down, it's cold out here.' She could see the warm flicker of firelight reflected in the varnished door.

'No. Get to the point, Julia.'

Julia's eyes fixed themselves on the third button of his crisp, white shirt. 'You know what the point is.'

'I want to hear it anyway,' unmoving and unmoved.

Julia licked her lips. Why was it so hard to say? *Because once you've said it he's going to shut the door on you again*, whispered the little know-it-all inside her head, *and you don't want him to shut you out, not ever*.

'It was all a mistake!' she rushed into speech to drown out that niggling thought. 'It wasn't meant for you—the cake, I mean, that's why I had to push you in the pool. Well, I suppose I didn't *have* to push you. Connie said I could have fainted, but I wasn't thinking straight. It's all Richard's fault, damn him!'

'Is this going to take long?' Hugh interrupted her string of disconnected remarks. 'I do have some work to do.'

'Will you shut up and listen!' Julia howled in exasperation, then clapped a hand over her stupid mouth, trying to get a grip on herself. She lowered it, staring him straight in the eye this time, determined: 'It would help if you stopped looking down your nose at me. I'm only trying to tell you how sorry I am.'

'At last. I accept your gracious apology, Julia. Good night.'

'No!' Julia grabbed at a solid forearm as he turned away. 'I haven't finished yet.'

'Oh? I distinctly heard you say you were sorry.'

'But I haven't told you *why*,' she wailed desperately.

Very carefully he removed her small, restraining hand—their only point of contact, thought Julia sadly. Her early desire to cry sneaked back and her face set. She rarely cried, and prided herself that she never sank to such emotional blackmail when reason failed. She blinked madly and tried for a casual shrug that fooled neither of them. They stared at each other for a moment, his rejection trembling in the air, then a stifled sigh broke from him and although his posture didn't change, the tension seemed to drain out of his face.

'I have a feeling I'm going to regret this ... but— why, Julia?'

The trace of gentleness in the soft, resigned voice, sent a flicker of pain through Julia. He was being kind because he felt sorry for her. She didn't want his pity any more than he would want hers. He was waiting, patiently, prepared for anything ... but not, it seemed for the Revenge of the Cake.

'My God!' The appalled exclamation was jerked from him as she reached the climax of her tale. 'Isn't one practical joker in the family enough?'

There was a tiny silence as they both absorbed the implications of his involuntary remark.

'In the family?' A small, tremulous smile lit Julia's wistful face. 'Was that a Freudian slip?'

'Since Freud is dead, and you, Julia, are a chef not a

psychologist, we'll have to forego the revelation.' Hugh
frowned repressively, but Julia's smile only widened as
she was swept by a marvellous wave of relief. It was
going to be all right, after all. She hadn't irreparably
damaged the tenuous threads of their relationship.

'I see I've been promoted again . . . back to chef,' she
exclaimed as he raised an eyebrow. 'Does that mean
that all is forgiven?'

'Did you think I would be so churlish as to say no?'

'Well, I wasn't sure,' Julia admitted frankly. 'You can
be awfully enigmatic when you try. You might have
thought it the perfect chance to get me the sack.'

His lids drooped concealingly. 'You don't have a very
high opinion of my good nature, do you?'

She smiled warmly at him, her happiness an ache in
her throat. 'Why don't I come in and we'll discuss all
your faults in detail . . . and mine of course.'

'I don't think so.' Firm but not dismissive, and this
time Julia didn't mind a bit.

'Another time, perhaps.'

'Perhaps. Good night, Julia.' So gravely polite, so
delightfully *Hughish* that she couldn't resist.

'Good night, Hugh. And thanks for being such a
darling about your dunking!' Going up on her tiptoes
she planted a laughing kiss on the highest reachable
point—the vulnerable spot where his strong throat
curved into his collarbone. The unexpected throb of his
pulse against her soft mouth imbued the kiss with a
disturbing intimacy and Julia whirled away from his
arrested gaze, breathless at her own temerity. Back in
the kitchen she attributed her slight giddiness to her
headlong rush down the stairs and had a snack to
revive herself.

Later, when Steve turned up for one of his late-night
chat sessions, Julia for once had little to say. Twice he
accused her of not listening to what he was saying and
the third time she was startled and upset when he
deliberately broke the glass he was holding to get her

attention. For one awful moment she thought he was going to throw the pieces at her, his white-faced anger all out of proportion to her crime. Hastily she had denied her indifference, but he had stormed out, leaving Julia to sweep up the shards of glass and wonder at his boiling frustration. On other nights she didn't even think he had cared about her divided attention.

Reluctantly Julia dragged herself out of bed and began to set her plans for the day afoot. At the appointed time she greeted Richard at the front door with a smug smile.

'We can't take the MG, Richard,' she said, noticing the keys in his hand. 'There won't be room.'

'Sure there will. The hamper'll fit in the boot.'

'But we won't.' Ros gave Julia a sly wink as she, Olivia and Steve carried the hamper through from the kitchen, and out to Steve's old Mark II Zephyr parked conveniently outside. Julia bit her lip to hold back a smile at Richard's annoyance as he trailed sulkily after them. That would teach him!

'Where's Charley? Don't tell me you didn't think to invite him, too?' he grumbled sourly in her ear.

'I did, but he didn't want to come. I've left him a packed lunch if that's what you're worried about,' said Julia with wicked relish as she climbed into the front seat alongside Steve. Charley was too wrapped up in his new project to want to go anywhere. He had already removed several vital, mysterious parts from the innards of the Beetle with a view to subjecting them to some complicated cleaning and lubricating process.

'Ready to go?' Steve gave her a pale smile.

To Julia's relief he seemed to have forgotten all about the previous night's tantrum. He seemed quite relaxed, almost sociable, so Julia didn't spoil the mood by mentioning it herself.

'Who on earth is this Logan person?' Julia asked Ros in a low voice as they unloaded the car at the beach. It seemed that every second sentence of Olivia's began: 'Logan thinks . . .' or 'Logan says . . .'.

Ros tossed her long hank of red hair over her shoulder with a contemptuous shrug. 'Haven't you heard of Logan Firth? Oh no, Olivia hadn't joined the commune the last time you saw us, had she? He's the founder . . . the ineffable guiding light. He's quite old—in his forties I think—but Livvy's well on the way to thinking herself in love with him. She's so naive about men . . . I'm hoping a few weeks under my mature influence might give her back her perspective.'

'You don't like him, obviously,' said Julia, amused by Ros' presumption of emotional superiority. Both seemed fairly level-headed twenty-one-year-olds as far as she was concerned.

'He's a pseud!' Ros declared. 'Do you know what his last exhibition was? He painted the gallery walls black and hung blank canvases on them.'

'Interesting,' murmured Julia provokingly.

'Come on, Ju! That sort of stuff only appeals to hard-core culture freaks. It doesn't take any real skill or imagination. Only audacity and ego.'

Privately Julia agreed. 'Just because you don't like his work doesn't mean that he's wrong for Olivia.'

'But he is!' The ardent feminist came to the crux of her argument. 'It's a farce to call that place a commune because it's not, it's an artistic dictatorship. Livvy doesn't need him—she's got more talent in her little finger than he has in his whole body. He's going to suffocate her with his gigantic ego . . . make her suffer artistically and emotionally.' She lowered her voice as Olivia headed up to collect her beach bag from the back seat. 'What's more he's a lecher and a hypocrite. He even made a pass at me! I bet he's had it off with every woman in that commune, yet he spouts on about woman's essential purity.'

'Olivia's got to make her own mistakes,' Julia offered wisely, while sympathising with Ros' attitude.

Ros sighed. 'I know, unfortunately. I wish I could get Hugh to talk to her.'

Julia's ears pricked up. 'I thought he didn't like to get involved in family turmoils.'

'He doesn't—that's the point. Only, when you *really* need him he won't turn you away. He sort of clarifies everything.'

'So why don't you tell him about Olivia?' Julia had noticed Hugh's talent for staying strictly neutral at dinner-time squabbles, illuminating all the stated points of view instead of stating his own.

'Livvy would kill me, that's why.'

Julia followed her frowningly down to the sand. The others could go to Hugh in need, but who did he turn to when he had problems? She couldn't imagine him sharing his doubts with anyone, he was too fiercely independent, too wary of involvement, lived far too much of his own life inside his skull. Last night she had sensed untapped depths of tenderness in him, and the unbidden thought came from nowhere: *what a wonderful father he would make, strong but gentle, kind but firm.*

There was no one else on the beach. The melon-rind of white sand was smooth and untasted. The girls squealed as they peeled off shoes and socks and paddled in the icy water. Only Richard was aloof, moodily skipping pebbles across the small, swelling waves. Julia, who never sulked, found his attitude childish and annoying. Ignoring him she turned to Steve:

'Fancy a walk before lunch? You're a history buff, aren't you? You can point out the spot where Captain Cook anchored the *Endeavour* in . . . when was it?'

Steve grinned. '1769. OK, history lesson coming up.' He raised his voice. 'Anyone else for a walk?' There were no takers and they began to stroll along the water-line, away from Richard's scowling stare.

'What's the matter with Rich?' asked Steve, when they were out of earshot. Julia was surprised. Until now his self-absorption had precluded interest in anyone else.

'He wanted this to be just the two of us.'

'Ah.' He caught on straight away. 'And you aren't buying?'

'I can't work out why Richard has suddenly developed this consuming passion for me,' Julia blurted out. 'We've been friends more or less for six years, if we were going to click we would have done so before now.'

'You know what Rich is like—he's prone to these sudden, intense enthusiasms.'

'Oh, yes, I know what he's like,' Julia said drily. 'That's one of the reasons I'm not interested. We used to have great fun together, but I can't enjoy his company if I'm having to slap him down all the time. I want to be friends again.'

Steve kicked at a lump of seaweed. 'He might actually be falling in love with you, have you considered that? You're bright, you're pretty, why shouldn't he?'

Julia brushed off the compliment. 'He's cried wolf once too often for me to believe that. I've seen him do this routine before—you know, the soulful looks, the poetic outbursts—but with other women. I never thought he'd be dumb enough to try it on me. No, he's just playing some game of his own ... unless ...' a thought occurred to her, '... unless it's frustration. I'm the only eligible female for miles, Richard's not used to such a dearth of prospects. Maybe it's his way of fighting withdrawal symptoms.'

Steve seemed to freeze beside her. She felt the physical change in him, the drawing in, the tension back in full force. They both stopped walking and Julia zipped up her leather jacket as her feet sank into the silky cool sand. Steve's thin, bony profile was screwed into an expression of pain as he watched the swooping glide of a gull above the estuary. There was a faint tic at the corner of his eye. Suddenly it all fell into place as Julia remembered ...

'Steve?'

He looked at her with hollow, haunted eyes and was still. 'You know, don't you.' It wasn't a question.

'I think so. I had a flatmate in London, a law student. She fell behind with her studies, then had to work twice as hard. She started taking things to keep her awake, then something else to make her sleep. Yet she still never seemed to make any ground.'

Steve gave a raw laugh of self-contempt. 'How well I know the feeling.'

'You're not . . .' Julia took a breath. 'It's not heroin, is it? You're just . . .'

' "Just"?' he repeated viciously. 'Oh, yes, I'm "just" uppers and downers. I thought I was being clever. I knew amphetamines weren't physically addictive, I thought I could handle the psychological side . . . I only needed them for a short time, you see, to get me through a bad patch. Classic tale, eh?'

It was, sadly so. 'How much are you taking,' Julia asked tentatively, remembering how Cathy had lashed out at attempts to help, but Steve seemed relieved that someone had guessed his burden.

He gave her a grim, death's-head smile. 'None, now. Why do you think I'm such a wreck? I haven't for three weeks. And it's not getting any easier!' The last was an agonised cry.

Words that had been dammed up for months came pouring out, Julia couldn't have stopped him if she had tried. Squeezed dry by the daily demands of rehearsal, recording, performance, Steve had resorted to drugs to fight off his exhaustion. Nights were spent writing music—all of *Hard Times'* material was original—and as time went by he had felt less and less able to produce the kind of music the rest of the group wanted. Then his voice showed signs of being affected by the strain and the drug-taking.

'We were committed to the hilt, I couldn't just take off for a few weeks' rest. That last Aussie tour I can't even remember what we did or where we went. It was like a bad dream. Since then I haven't been able to write anything worth a dime. I can't think, I can't concentrate and it's getting to the stage where I'm afraid to even try.'

'Does anyone else know?' It was possible they didn't. The lack of appetite, ultra-sensitive nerves, alternate bouts of restlessness and lethargy could all be attributed to simple stress.

'The guys . . . how could they help it? We live on top of each other most of the time, especially when we're on tour. But nobody here, and I don't want them to know, Julia,' he said urgently, the second member of the family to seek confidence of her, 'it's something I have to handle myself.'

Pointless to say that it was because he hadn't sought help that he had got himself into this mess in the first place. 'Not even Richard?'

'Especially not Rich. He's always been the stronger one, the dominant one. He'd help all right, but he wouldn't *understand*. Rich would never touch drugs, for any reason, none of them would. I have to do this myself. If I don't, then I haven't beaten it, it's just exchanging one crutch for another.'

He was so wrong, but Julia knew from experience that there was little she could say to persuade him otherwise. It wasn't his family's shock, or disapproval, or lack of understanding he couldn't face, it was his own sense of guilt and shame.

'Three weeks, though, that's good isn't it?' she asked gently, careful to be optimistic rather than pitying.

'Is it?' he searched her small, compassionate face intently. 'I hope to God it is. I hope it doesn't get any worse. I'm so damned scared. I've never been so scared in my life. I have to do it, I have to make it, but I don't know if I can.' He took a half-sobbing, desperate breath and Julia moved to put her arms around him, hugging him fiercely, protectively, feeling a strong maternal urge

at his helplessness. It seemed as though she could feel
every bone in his body, tense and trembling. Above
their heads a gull mewed plaintively.

'You'll do it, I'm certain you will,' she told him with
soft conviction. 'I think you should tell Michael and
Connie, they love you, they accept you as you are. But
if you can't . . . and things get too bad—there's always
me.'

Steve pulled back, eyes glistening greenly, and cupped
her face within his hands. 'Thank you for that. I don't
know why I can talk to you when I can't to anyone else,
but thanks. Now I know why Rich has such a passion
for you. You're a sweet and lovely lady, and I'm a
bastard for hassling you last night.'

He kissed her, a vastly different kiss from the kind his
brother had given her. This was one of hungry
desperation, searching for certainty and Julia submitted,
unable to reject his fragile faith.

She followed his lead as they slowly made their way
back to the others, responding to his transparent
attempts to lighten the mood, and they were laughing as
they threw themselves down on the rug to tackle the
food. Coy little comments from Ros and Olivia, and
more moroseness from Richard soon made it clear that
they had all seen that kiss. Ordinarily Julia would have
tried to smooth things over, but it occurred to her that
here was the way to show Richard she wasn't interested.
Steve seemed to realise what she was doing and obliged
by playing up beautifully. They exchanged frequent
secret smiles and Steve came protectively to her aid
against Richard's disgruntled digs.

It was only a few days later that she realised where
her foolishness had landed her. Now she had *both* twins
competing for her attention, each with the semblance of
sincerity, each equally intent on thwarting the other.
Julia, unsure of Steve's motives, was afraid to try and
shake him off with the same ruthlessness she used with
Richard. His skin was particularly thin at the moment,

who knew how he would take it if she appeared to withdraw her support?

Reduced to trying to avoid one quarter of the household Julia slipped out the back door one morning, intending to escape on a little shopping expedition on her own. It wasn't until she saw her incomplete VW that she remembered her predicament. She heard Richard's voice calling her in the kitchen and belted around the side of the house, almost straight into the path of the Maserati.

'Are you going to the store? Could you give me a lift?' she panted hopefully through the window.

'I'm going in to Whitianga,' Hugh replied smoothly.

'Oh.' Julia looked at him and he sighed.

'Can you do your shopping in Whitianga?'

'Terrific!' Julia scrambled in beside him as he released the handbrake. 'But I'll have to be back to get lunch.'

'I'm at your command.'

Julia grinned at his dryness. 'Quite like old times, isn't it?' She turned to wave out of the window as they passed an open-mouthed Richard.

'I hope not,' came the reply, with soft fervency.

'I wasn't that bad, was I?'

'You . . . were Julia.'

'You make me sound like a noxious pest.'

'Not noxious. Obnoxious, perhaps.'

'Are you making a joke?' she asked, astounded.

'I never joke, Julia, you told me so yourself. I don't know how to laugh.'

'That's not fair, I apologised for all that,' Julia protested, flooded with renewed guilt about what she had said to him. 'Anyway, I've changed my mind about that, you do have a sense of humour . . . somewhere.' She decided a change of subject was also in order. 'You know it was really this car that threw me off the track the day we met. I couldn't believe that the brother Richard described could drive a Maserati.'

'How did Richard describe me?' Mildly amused.

'Oh . . . Mercedes, BMW . . .'

'Ah . . . solid, dependable, Teutonic.'

'Certainly not a rich and dashing Italian.'

'Do you always deal in superficialities?'

'Only when they're all I have to go on,' Julia shot back. 'What does the G. B. stand for? Not Grevious Bodily by any chance?'

A slight twitch of the straight mouth showed that he followed the reference. 'George Bernard.'

'Was your mother a Shaw fan?'

'I doubt that she ever read a play in her life.'

Julia hesitated, considering the inadvisability of probing the flat statement any further. Was that resentment towards his mother that she detected? Had she been lacking in intellect, or just uneducated? Julia badly wanted to know, but the desire to shield him from summoning ugly memories was stronger.

'I like Hugh,' she said quietly. 'It's just the name for a large man.'

'You are obsessed by my size, aren't you,' he murmured, hand moving to change down gear fluidly as he approached a corner.

'I know, I can't help it. I've had some traumatic experiences with big men.' She told him about the enormous Italian she had worked for in Rome, the one who kept pinching her.

'You needn't fear that from me.'

'I know.' He wasn't a man who encouraged any kind of familiarity. 'I bet you don't go much for small women, anyway. I bet all your girlfriends are tall and slim and keep their hands in their laps like Miss Farrow.'

'Let's keep Ann out of this, shall we?'

'I think she thought I had a crush on you and was trying to attract your attention by the pool,' said Julia, and pounced on a tiny change of expression. 'She did, didn't she? Did she say something afterwards . . . delicately of course . . . to suggest I shouldn't be enouraged in my infatuation?'

'Julia. . . .'

'She did!' Julia could laugh about it now. 'I hope you were horribly pompous in reply.'

'What did you do about Signor Gianelli?'

'Who? Oh . . .' she smiled, successfully diverted. 'I threw a plate of Spaghetti Marinara at him one night, but he ducked and it hit his wife. She was fat too, but she didn't have much of a sense of humour. She fired me in front of the whole restaurant, but at least I still had my self-respect. I was given a standing ovation as I—*stop the car!*'

'What's the matter, are you ill?' But he obeyed her immediately, swivelling to look at her, sharp-eyed. 'Are you all right?'

'You smiled!' she breathed, full of the discovery. 'I've never seen you do it before.'

'I can hardly grin like a maniac all the time just for your benefit. Is that why I stopped the car?'

'You don't look in the least like a maniac. You looked rather cute.' Julia wasn't to be diverted again.

This time she received it head on and she stared in fascination. His whole face changed, eyes crinkling endearingly at the edges, the grey irises hazing into blue, like a sunwarmed sky after a rainshower. His smile was slightly crooked, revealing the fullness of his lower lip and straight, even teeth. It was a beautiful, masculine smile, one that made you want to smile back, and keep on smiling.

Julia could hardly believe the difference it made to this careful, controlled man and it further strengthened her belief that he was worth cultivating. She wouldn't be satisfied with a nodding acquaintanceship with his strange, complex personality. She wanted more, more perhaps than he was willing to offer, but it was unthinkable that she should retreat now to the safe, uncontroversial distance that he kept everyone else at. She had trespassed this far, and now she must cling to her advantage.

'Admit it,' she teased softly, with more confidence than she felt. 'Under that grizzly skin is hidden a sweet ole honey bear.'

He restarted the engine, casting her a brooding glance as if he sensed her purpose. 'Don't you ever give up?'

'Nope. I may be small, but I'm sassy!'

'I had noticed.'

They drove on, Julia content to let the conversation take a less personal turn. She felt she had achieved a major victory. They were no longer locked into that circle of challenge and counter challenge, now a new element had entered their relationship. She found herself liking his articulate intelligence. He was talking to her as an equal, and what a difference it made!

They parted by the Post Office and arranged to meet in an hour at the wharf.

'While I'm here I may as well stock up on some fresh fish, if you don't mind, said Julia, taking it for granted that he wouldn't. She wandered around the nearly empty streets of the quiet town, making a number of small purchases before strolling in the direction of a circling cloud of seagulls that told her one of the fishing boats had arrived.

She was skilfully haggling over a small box of shiny-eyed schnapper and some very active crayfish when Hugh found her. He didn't join her immediately but watched from a distance, his bulk leant on an iron bollard, as she carried on a subtle flirtation with the fisherman. Long experience in the markets had taught Julia that men didn't resent a woman's hard bargaining if it was leavened with good-humoured repartee. Ros's hair would stand on end, but Julia enjoyed it in the same spirit as her adversaries.

'Do you always operate like that?' Hugh asked as he helped her with her bargains.

'Why not? I've got the equipment!' She put the plastic bucket of crays into the boot of the Maserati. 'I hope you don't mind if your car smells a bit fishy for a while.'

'Do I have a choice?'

'I could always put my thumb out,' she said, tongue in cheek. 'There are people who would pick me up, fish and all.'

'As you say, you have the equipment.'

Julia looked at him quickly, wondering if he was smiling again. His face was bland. 'You have a body too you know, everybody uses non-verbal language.'

'But not quite so blatantly as you.'

'Rubbish!' scoffed Julia. 'You're as blatant as Mt Egmont, without even moving. You just stand and stare and the rest of us quail.'

'I hope you don't have the audacity to include yourself in that "us".'

'No, well, I think we've already agreed I have a big mouth.'

Hugh had his hand on the key in the ignition, but before he turned it he looked at her, his eyes dropping involuntarily to her mouth as she spoke. It definitely wasn't big, though her lips were full, the upper lip a perfect bow even without an outlining of lipstick. She felt an uncharacteristic surge of self-consciousness as he stared at her and moistened her lips one against the other as if she could hide them from his gaze. The grey eyes rose to meet her startled blue ones and for an instant Julia saw masculine curiosity. He looked away and the moment was gone but she was left with a quickening sense of excitement that dismayed her. He was so big, so strong, so controlled ... not at all the kind of man who attracted her.

He drove faster on the way home, but still safely, with margin for other people's errors and Julia gradually relaxed as the talk remained amiable. So confident was she that he had begun to revise his former opinion of her that she wasn't offended when the conversation turned to his family and he remarked on the way she was playing Richard and Steve off against each other.

'I'm not playing, they are,' she shrugged. 'They don't need any encouragement from me.'

'Come on, Julia, flirting is as natural to you as breathing. Some active discouragement might help.'

The unfairness of it irked. She couldn't very well be rude to the twins when the rest of the family were there. Certainly when she was on her own she tried the usually successful ploy of not taking them seriously. Hugh didn't know the complications involved with Steve. 'Some men don't need either,' she said darkly. 'Some men take a woman's mere presence as flirtation. What should I do, wear a gag and mask!'

'It might make life a little more peaceful for the rest of us,' replied Hugh, with infuriating calm. 'More to the point, why don't you make up your mind which one you really want and put the other out of his misery.'

That was a bit strong. 'I don't want either of them,' Julia protested. 'And they don't really want me. It's just a game.'

'It may be a game to you, but to them it's real.' The soft voice held a hint of contempt at her blindness. 'Don't you feel the animosity between them? That's new. They may have bickered and fought in the past, but this is the first time there's been any real acrimony in it. If it goes any further I think you're in danger of permanently damaging their relationship.'

'You're exaggerating, it's not that bad,' said Julia, springing to her own defence despite her niggle of doubt. 'They're twins . . .'

'You obviously don't know them as well as you think you do. There's always been competitiveness between them—that's partly I think why they were determined not to go in the same profession—certainly they are close but they are two people, not one, and in the last couple of years they've become even more different. If you're serious about not wanting either of them, I suggest you make it crystal clear, now, before the tension escalates beyond a manageable level.'

Julia bit her lip, staring straight ahead as she remembered what Steve had said about Richard being the dominant one. Was Hugh right? Was he seeing all the angles this time, the ones Julia was too close to see?

'Richard's not serious, he can't be,' she said weakly. 'Have you ever known him to be serious about anything?'

'Yes. His work,' said Hugh with clipped precision.

'What's that got to do with me?'

'Don't be obtuse, Julia. Richard's technique is to live his roles and what's he playing next? He's Romeo and he's cast you as Juliet. He's in the process of genuinely convincing himself that he's in love with you.'

Julia gulped. What incredible logic. And incredibly, it fitted exactly Richard's behaviour, explained away his sudden attachment to her. Why, only yesterday, out on the upper balcony helping Jean beat carpets, she had been serenaded with the most famous lines of them all—'what light through yonder window breaks'. He had done the whole scene, oblivious to her rudely inappropriate responses. Hugh, having given her time to mull it over, was speaking again:

'As to Steve. It's quite obvious to all of us that he is at a vulnerable point in a personal crisis. I suppose you've been letting him cry on your shoulder.'

Was he always right, about everything! 'What if I have?'

'Don't let your sympathy go too far ... or has it already? It's very easy to confuse it with love, particularly if you're as confused to start with as Steve is.'

'What do you suggest I do?' gritted Julia resentfully, forgetting their earlier harmony. 'Turn my back?'

'Curb your natural instincts perhaps.'

'Why you infuriating, pompous, arrogant ...' Julia exploded, temper fueled by his apparent calm. 'You have a nerve! How dare you insinuate that I go around seducing everything that moves. I do have some discrimination you know, witness my attitude to you!'

'Let it drop, Julia, I don't think this discussion is getting us anywhere.'

'It's getting me somewhere. It's getting me mad,' Julia cried at the unmoved profile. 'And don't think you can shut me up with a snub. You ought to inspect your own back yard. Maybe if *you* offered Steve some sympathetic attention he wouldn't turn to me. Maybe if *you* got involved instead of standing on the side-lines sneering at the rest of us you could help. But will you? Oh no, that's not your style. You don't like getting involved, even with your own family—'

'That's enough, Julia.'

'No it's not enough. Richard was right, you get away with too much. They *care* about you, the least you can do is care about them.' She glared at him until the silence got too much for her. 'And why don't you argue back, damnit, instead of sitting there like a stuffed dummy.'

'I'm driving the car,' he replied mildly. 'And I thought it was a stuffed shirt?'

'A stuffed dummy in a stuffed shirt,' Julia yelled wildly. 'If your eyes didn't move I wouldn't know you were alive. Where is your life, Hugh? In your law books? Up in that attic prison? With well-oiled brunette robots—'

Fortunately she was interrupted. 'We're here, Julia.' She hadn't even noticed the car had stopped. She flung out of the car, pushing him out of the way as he came around to help her. 'I notice you don't call it home— that's because you don't know the meaning of the word. You don't know about love, either, so don't preach to me on the subject. Don't you tell me how to run my life . . .'

'You're telling me how to run mine,' he finally sounded fed up, and Julia was fed up too. Angrily she slammed the car door and would have stormed away but for the grunting moan he gave. She felt faint with shock as she realised she had slammed the door on his fingers.

'Oh my God,' she whispered, wrenching the door
open again and catching sight of the three middle
fingers of his left hand. They were white and crumpled;
in places the skin was broken and as the blood rushed
back into the injured fingers it began to drip out onto
the gravel in a steady stream. Julia watched aghast as
dark blood welled up under the nails—the pain must be
excruciating! She reached to help. 'Here, let me . . .'

'Don't touch me!' howled Hugh, back away, following
it up with a savage. 'Don't even come near me.'

'You'd better come into the kitchen, quickly,'
croaked Julia, alarmed by his agonised white face. 'I'll
put some ice on them, it'll help the pain.'

'I'll do it myself,' he ground out, and began to walk
stiffly towards the house, cradling his damaged hand in
his right.

'I'm sorry, Hugh, I was so angry I didn't think,' Julia
pleaded, trotting to keep up with him.

'You never do. Where in God's name am I safe from
you?'

'In the kitchen,' said Julia automatically, almost in
tears at her helplessness. 'I never have accidents there.
Please . . .'

They had reached the back door. Hugh stopped and
swung around on her, forestalling her offer. 'No! Go
away, Julia. Just GO AWAY.'

'I won't hurt you, I promise. What are you afraid of?'

He looked her up and down. 'Death!' he said,
succinctly, and strode inside, shutting the door. Julia
hovered for a few minutes, aching to go in; make up in
some way for her carelessness, but she didn't dare. She
made herself go back to the car and unload her
shopping, feeling a little sick herself as she remembered
those poor crushed fingers.

'Julia? What's the matter?' She turned to see Michael
Marlow climbing easily out of the large, low window of
his study. 'You look like a tragedy queen. What's
happened? Where's Hugh?'

'I shut his fingers in the car door,' Julia wailed, glad for somebody to confess her guilt to.

'Is he all right?' asked Michael, concerned.

'He won't let me near him,' Julia complained sadly. 'He shut me out of the kitchen.'

'Well, if he's ambulant it can't be too bad,' he replied consolingly. 'Don't take it so hard, Julia, he was the same as a boy. If ever he was hurt he used to retreat like an animal, it took years for Connie to convince him to accept comfort, but I'm afraid the habit of stoicism is deeply ingrained. I'll check on him later, if you like. You look a bit green yourself, come into the study and have a shot of brandy.'

He made to go back through the window but Julia was stricken to the spot by the thought of Hugh suffering his torment in silence and loneliness. 'I keep doing these terrible things to him,' she mourned, and then, the final straw. 'He shouted at me, he thinks I'm trying to kill him!' She could hold back no longer. Right there, in the middle of the driveway, with a bucket of crayfish clacking at her feet, she burst into tears.

Michael, who had lived and worked with volatile women all his life, took it in his stride. He let her bawl loudly into his sympathetic shoulder while he absently patted her head—and wondered . . .

CHAPTER SIX

HUGH didn't come down to dinner that night. Visions of him starving on his bed of pain were banished by Michael, who sidled up to her after supper and informed Julia out of the corner of his mouth that the patient, bandaged and aspirined, had his nose back to the grindstone.

'Is he in much pain?' she ventured fearfully.

'He didn't say ... he was a mite bad-tempered, though, when I enquired.'

Julia could imagine. 'Oh, why do I get myself into these things,' she moaned, guilty all over again.

'Swings and roundabouts, Julia,' Michael told her calmly. 'You're in the pink with the rest of my sons.'

Little did he know, thought Julia, sinking deeper into gloom. With Charley, sure, but she was fed up with the other two. And their antics over the next few days only strained relations even further. Hugh had been right, damn him, but it was too late to heed his advice. Romeo was revelling in his hot-headed temperament and Steve had decided that it was his duty in life to protect Julia from his 'shop-soiled Casanova' of a brother. The game of one-upmanship had got totally out of hand.

What worried Julia most was that Steve might be transferring some of his dependence to her ... using her as the kind of crutch that he had so adamantly rejected as being no cure at all. He had regained some of his old fire, and had even furtively begun composing again ('it's dedicated to you, Julia love') but the demons still lurked close by. How was she supposed to wriggle out from between the twins and still leave their pride and feelings intact? She didn't want to have to forfeit her friendship with them by being brutal. If only she had listened to Hugh, instead of leaping down his throat, she might have nipped things in the bud!

One afternoon, in a fit of grim determination, Julia accepted an invitation to accompany Richard and Steve to Hot Water Beach, intending to make a last-ditch effort to reconcile the brothers. She sat between them in the front seat of Steve's Zephyr and kept up a rolling chatter that drowned out the occasional snidery from either side and when they reached the beach she obediently carried the towels while the twins forged ahead, shovels in hand, to find the right spot. This, of course, meant another argument.

The tide was at its lowest ebb and a sharp breeze swept up the wide slope of the beach, buffeting their warmly clad bodies with cold as they finally selected a site just below the high-tide line. Even in this they have to compete, thought Julia with a sigh, as she watched the furious way in which the twins set to their task. As the hole deepened, steam began to rise, to be whipped away by the breeze, and the water beg an to seep at quickening rate. Julia took off her boots and thick socks and dipped her toe into the gathering pool.

'Ouch, it's hot!' She pulled a face when there was no answer from the dogged workers. As they widened and deepened the rapidly filling pool Julia took the towels up to the protective overhang of a towering clay and rock cliff and stripped down to her magenta bikini. The short dash back down the beach raised a good crop of goosepimples.

She murmured with sensuous pleasure as she lowered herself into the water, stretched out full-length in the silky hotness. The combination of heat and cold was delicious and Julia could see from her cosy cocoon that there were a few other people dotted around the beach in the pattern of the heated underflows, enjoying themselves in the same way. If it were summer they would all be making intermittent forays into the cooling waves of the Pacific Ocean.

Richard and Steve went up to pull off their clothes and came racing back, stride for stride. Richard won the place beside Julia, but Steve got his revenge by taking the other end and thrusting his legs back up between them. Julia pretended not to notice the sly jostlings as she rehearsed her little speech.

'OK you two, I've got something to say,' she launched into the glaring silence. 'I didn't come here to watch you two sit and scowl at each other . . .'

'I'm not scowling—he is,' objected Richard immediately. 'If you'll remember, *I* was the one who suggested this little outing. I didn't ask *him* to come along and get on everybody's nerves with his self-pitying sulks.'

'*I'm* not the one who gets on Julia's nerves,' Steve snapped back. 'It's your hammy sentimentality that's driving her crazy . . . quoting all those second-hand emotions as if she was another one of your gullible groupies.' A kick received a vicious jab in exchange. They were deaf to Julia's entreaties and she was beginning to feel desperate.

'Why don't you ask *me* what I want for a change, instead of telling each other what you want me to want?' she demanded winding herself up to a righteous anger.

'Enjoying yourselves?'

Three faces gaped out of the nest of steam. Hugh! his bulk increased by a thick coat, collar turned up against the wind.

'Fantastic!' said Richard, acting for all he was worth.

'Great!' said Steve, not to be outdone.

Julia said nothing. She just sat there, mouth open, looking like a tiny seductive siren. Pale curves glimmered under the light covering of water, her full, rounded breasts, supported by thin straps of magenta, gleamed invitingly. Creamy shoulders barely broke the surface of the steam-kissed water and her blonde hair, darkened by dampness, curled closely around her small, flushed face.

'What are you doing here? Is something wrong?' asked Julia anxiously as she got over her initial surprise.

'Urgent messages.'

'Who for?' chorused the twins hopefully.

'Zak ...' Steve bit his lip in annoyance at the mention of his manager's name while Richard grinned triumphantly, '... wants to talk to Steve. Something about technical problems with the new album—some of the tracks may have to be re-laid.'

'Can't it wait?' asked Steve. There was no sign of panic on his face and Julia let out a small, unnoticed sigh. He really *was* putting the past few months behind him, although he hadn't fully realised it yet.

'Not according to Zak,' replied Hugh, stripping off his brown leather gloves and thrusting them into his coat pocket. 'And there was one for you, too, Richard.' The grin was wiped off as if by a sponge. 'Your film company. The director wants to hear from you, as of an hour ago. Schedule changes, I believe. Olivia can tell you more—she took the calls.'

'Damn!' A brief struggle, which ambition won. 'Do you mind awfully, Juliet, if we go back?' said Richard in his best wheedling tone. 'We could come back tomorrow, or another day?'

Julia opened her mouth, aware of relief.

'There's no need for Julia to go,' inserted Hugh smoothly. 'She can go back with me, later. No sense in spoiling her afternoon as well as yours.'

'But ...'

'But ...'

It was the first time Julia had ever seen both twins lost for words simultaneously. It was a sight to behold.

'Julia doesn't mind, do you?'

'Er ... no ... no,' she said flabbergasted by his

apparent friendliness. 'I'd like to stay,' she added, more firmly.

'That's settled, then,' said Hugh. 'Run along, boys, I'll look after your girlfriend.'

He smiled his honey-bear smile at Julia and she, who had missed it lately, smiled back. The twins retreated in disarray, actually talking civilly to each other as they went.

'Thanks.' Julia looked ruefully up at the hard-boned faced crowned by a vast grey sky. 'It was going to be pistols at dawn next.'

'I did warn you.'

'I know. Hey!' as he began moving away. 'Where are you going? You're not going to leave me stranded, are you?' She sat up hurriedly, water cascading down between her breasts. Hugh's gaze wavered, and steadied on her face.

'I'm merely going up there,' he pointed to where the twins were towelling off and dressing, 'to take off my clothes.'

'But you can't do that!' cried a scandalised Julia.

'I've dressed and undressed myself ever since I was four years old,' he replied patiently and then made a gesture of mock enlightenment with his large hands. 'Oh, I see what you mean. I *am* wearing swimming togs. And I might add that they're a lot more modest than those two strips of nothing you're pretending to wear.'

'Stuffy!' Julia threw after him, when she recovered from her blush, aware that her unthinking cry had emanated from her subconscious, that unruly desire to see what Hugh was like underneath his civilised wrappings.

She swopped ends so she could watch him coming back down the beach and returned the twins' reluctant farewell waves with a cheery one of her own. It only took Hugh a few minutes to divest himself of his clothes and Julia took a deep breath at the sight of him bearing down on her. Steady on, my girl, she told herself, you don't like big men. But she liked the look of this one.

His swimming togs might be more modest than hers
in terms of amount of material, but they certainly
weren't modest *per se*. The sleek, clinging, racing briefs
in red which seemed to accentuate rather than cloak, his
manhood, riding high at the top of the solid columns of
muscle that were his legs. Shorn of his clothing he was
definitely not shorn of his power! Julia sternly quelled a
sudden urge to escape the approaching colossus, and
concentrated instead on admiring his symmetry.

No wonder he was so hard to bump into—the flat,
broad stomach was rippled with muscle, the high arch
of his rib-cage supporting a deep chest and powerful
shoulders. Each pace threw a different set of muscles
into relief on his body, solid-packed yet beautifully
proportioned as a whole. His skin was much paler than
Julia's but dark hair covered the strong forearms and
legs and rode the muscles of his chest. There was a fine
covering of hair in a line from his indented navel,
thickening as it disappeared under the red nylon astride
his hips. If he had been a friend, or merely an
acquaintance of her own age, Julia would have wolf-
whistled, but she contented herself with giving Hugh an
approving sweep of her lashes . . . this time.

He slid easily into the water and Julia felt the long
length of his leg slide momentarily along her softly
rounded one. Hard and soft. Julia felt a shiver of self-
awareness. It seemed much more intimate sharing the
pool with one large man, than it had with two,
bickering boys.

The breeze had died in the interim and a light rain
began to fall, little more than a mist, to mingle with the
steam. Julia let her head fall back so that she could
taste the sweet purity as it descended on them.

'Mmmm lovely. I hope it doesn't cool us down too
much.' She lifted her tangled lashes to find herself
under study. 'Aren't you glad you came?' she teased.
'Exactly why did you come, and not Olivia, if she took
the messages?'

'I offered to come. I happened to be downstairs, taking a break.'

Julia's eyes went uncertainly to the taped hand he was taking care not to dip in the water. Hugh? Taking a break? Unheard of! 'Is your hand bothering you?'

'Among other things.' He didn't elaborate as to what they were. 'It throbs a little.' His lids drooped until his eyes were mere grey slits. 'Michael tells me that you cried all over him that morning.'

'I thought I'd wet someone else's suit for a change,' Julia grinned at him, unembarrassed. 'I was sorry for being such an idiot and you wouldn't let me relieve my feelings by helping you. You really were quite beastly about it. I was worried that you might be left-handed and not able to write at all.'

'I'm right-handed. However, my manuscript to date has been typed.'

'Oh.' And: 'Ooohh,' as it sank in. 'How long before you can use your fingers do you think?'

'A week at least. They're pretty badly bruised.'

'Oh.' She moved uneasily, creating tiny ripples in the water, aware that Hugh was watching her in a narrow, assessing way, uncertain of what he expected her to do.

'Well, it'll do you good to take it easy for a while,' she said. 'It's done me good already . . . you were free to gallop to my rescue. I should have taken your advice days ago; now Richard and Steve are so wrapped up in the business of scoring off each other that they've forgotten all about listening to me. Why are you looking at me like that?'

'You're admitting that I was right?'

'Why shouldn't I?' she demanded. 'You were. If you'd put it more delicately I would have agreed with you at the time, and maybe avoided all this.'

'So now it's my fault.'

'It's nobody's fault, just an unfortunate set of circumstances.' Julia gave a baffled sigh. 'Richard's always ear-bashing me about The Method . . . you have

to live a part to make it believable ... I would have
clicked sooner if I hadn't been so busy wondering
whether it was one of his damned practical jokes. And
as for Steve ...' she hesitated and made a quick
decision. It wouldn't be a betrayal of trust, since Hugh
was the one member of the family on whom she could
rely not to rush in with an excess of sympathy. He
listened thoughtfully, the broad angles of his face
sloping austerely as she told him about Steve's struggle,
and her own fears about rejecting him.

'I think he's tougher, more resilient, than you give him
credit for. After all, the initial decision to stop was his.'

'Maybe,' Julia admitted having the same thoughts
herself. 'If only I could find a graceful way to withdraw
that wouldn't damage his self-esteem. I can't favour one
of them at the expense of the other, that'll only get me
in deeper. What they need is a short, sharp, painless
shock.' She paused, expectantly.

'Are you *asking* me?' said Hugh, after a moment. 'I
wouldn't like to provoke another violent reaction with
gratuitous advice, I only have one undamaged hand
left.'

The rain was beginning to come down a little more
heavily and Julia was fascinated by the way the drops
channelled themselves down the grooves in Hugh's face,
and the muscular indentations in his neck and shoulders.
They both lounged lower in the water, Hugh's
bandaged hand immersed to the base of its thumb, like
a white marker buoy bobbing on the surface. Julia
wondered what excuse he'd given to the rest of the
family ... he must have been blessedly vague about the
reason for his injury, for no one had questioned Julia.

'Well?'

Julia shook her head slightly, wishing she wasn't
quite so aware of his physical presence, so disturbed by
it. 'Yes, I'm asking you.'

'Perhaps you could introduce another man on to the
scene.'

'*Another* one.' Julia was appalled. 'That would be just compounding the problem.'

'Not if he was tame, and impressive enough to stop the twins in their tracks, permanently.'

His eagle eyes missed none of her puzzlement. She had the definite feeling that this was all leading somewhere, but she couldn't fathom the reason. It wasn't at all what she had expected from him. 'Perhaps you can tell me where I'm going to find a spare man around here? There's Charley, of course, but I wouldn't like to be accused of cradle snatching. There *are* no other men.'

'Thank you,' so drily as to crackle like an onion skin.

'What? Oh,' Julia giggled. 'You know what I mean.'

'I don't think I do. Are you suggesting that I am not a man?'

'No . . . er . . . what I meant was no other *suitable* men.'

'What makes me unsuitable, apart from my size, of course?'

Julia turned her face up to the rain and laughed. Her whole body shimmered with it, creating interesting patterns in the water. 'You and me?' she gasped. 'What a ridiculous thought!' She was too contorted with laughter to see the strange expression slide across his face.

'I knew you found me amusing, I didn't know you also found me ridiculous.'

'Not you . . . us.' Julia unsuccessfully fought her giggles. 'Can you just imagine it. Come on, Hugh, even you have to admit it's funny.'

'I'm not laughing.'

Julia hiccupped to a stop. 'No, I can see that,' she said in a voice that trembled. She pressed a hand over her mouth and a series of snorts and snuffles were emitted as tear-blurred blue eyes squinted with laughter.

'Keep on laughing at me, Julia, and I might feel impelled to show you just how unfunny I can be.'

Julia sobered, almost, at the dangerous softness of his words. Without moving one magnificent muscle he was suddenly all affronted masculinity. She felt as if she had drifted out into the wide Pacific without a compass, so unexpected was this reaction from Hugh. 'You weren't serious, though, were you,' she ventured carefully.

'No?' He gave a new kind of smile, small and threatening, that sent a tingle across Julia's scalp.

'But you can't be,' she protested, no longer laughing. 'You and me? Nobody would believe it. I wouldn't believe it! Not after what's happened between us so far. It's absurd, it's . . .' she stopped herself from saying 'ridiculous' just in time.

'Why? Haven't you ever heard of the attraction of opposites. We've been fighting against it, now we've given in. We can make it believable. My family is stuffed to the gills with romance; they'll believe what they want to believe.'

Scepticism was stamped firmly all over Julia's features as she stared at him. Was he finally cracking up?'

'Are you having me on? Is this to pay me back for your hand? You can't seriously mean that you and I should pretend to be mad about each other,' her voice rose and cracked at the high note. Another giggle squeezed out of the crack and Julia gave a small scream as Hugh made a sudden lunging turn in the confined space, like the splashing charge of a big 'gator. A thick fore-arm pressed against her collarbone, across her throat, stilling her in place while the other, injured hand, was supported by his elbow on the sandy bank. His face was close enough for her to see the firm, resilient texture of his pale skin, stretched across the bones of his skull like fine, expensive leather. Julia tried to slide down under his arm, but her way was blocked by a broad chest and the clamp of a powerful leg over hers.

'Hugh, what are you doing!' Julia was shocked and

excited at the same time. Hadn't she secretly wondered what it would be like to touch that muscle-padded body, to admire it with her fingers as well as with her eyes?

'Wiping the smile off your face,' came the implacable reply. 'I ... don't ... like ... being ... laughed at.' His words were punctuated by small nips in a line down her vulnerable throat from her ear.

'Hugh!' Julia squealed. This had to be a fantasy, it couldn't be happening, though goodness knows why she should conjure up Hugh in a fantasy ... why not Warren Beatty, or Robert Redford? 'You'll only make me laugh more, I'm ticklish—especially on my neck.'

The great grey head lifted and Julia could have sworn he was laughing ... it had to be a fantasy! 'You would be,' he sighed. 'What about your mouth, is that ticklish?'

She couldn't answer; he was kissing her, lips parted and parting hers. She forgot all about laughing, about where she was and who *he* was. She was too busy making the startling discovery that she was enjoying his technique.

Oh well, I may as well make the best of it, she thought hazily and she lowered her long, brown lashes and tilted her mouth under his, inviting him further. For a moment she felt his muscles bunch, then she felt his chest settle lightly against her, the thick curling wet hairs caressing the swell of her breasts. The pressure came off her collarbone as a large hand slid around to the nape of her neck and down, to the centre of her back as he lifted her softly against him.

Julia put her hands on his shoulders, feeling the shifting strength, the smooth, slick wetness of curving muscle. His lips and teeth and tongue were excitingly active, tugging gently at the soft inner skin of her mouth, exciting her taste-buds, drawing her own small tongue into the depths of his dark mouth with gentle sucking motions that were incredibly erotic. All sensation was centred on her face, but she was gradually becoming aware of his hand splayed on her spine, the hard stomach pressing against the ridge of her hip.

Hugh made a deep sound of satisfaction which reverberated in his chest, vibrating the water around Julia so that she felt totally immersed in him, part of him. His explorative, explosive kiss changed tempo, his tongue making tiny, swift, stabbing forays into her mouth. Julia's hands slid up into the amazingly soft dampness of his grey hair, feeling the short strands slip strokingly through her fingers as she gripped, trying to stop those erotically frustrating withdrawals. In the water she felt weightless, he felt weightless on her and he was so incredibly gentle for his size, touching and stroking delicately, the big hands both firm and controlling, yet tender.

Suddenly it was over and Julia sighed, opening her eyes wide, unable to believe it had really happened and that she had reacted so strongly. 'Where on earth did you learn to kiss like that?'

'Didn't you like it?'

He had to be kidding! 'Did you get a degree in kissing, as well as law, at university?'

He rolled sideways, staring at the small face alight with pleasure and mischief, flushed with heat, and something else.

'Do I get an A for believability?' he countered drily and Julia winced imperceptibly. She preferred to think that the kiss had been unplanned, an impulse from an unimpulsive man.

'OK, so I admit that, kissing-wise at least, we might be able to carry it off.' A part of her noticed with interest that the tips of his ears had a faint pink tinge. Perhaps she had discovered the secret of reading his emotions—an ear-indicator as it were. Did it mean that he wasn't as unmoved as he appeared to be? She continued, with a slight frown. 'But what do you get out of it? I can't believe you're offering out of the goodness of your heart.'

'I . . .' he looked down, encountered the intriguing curves and tucks of three magenta triangles and flicked the grey eyes hurriedly up again, emptied of expression. 'I need your help.'

'Help? You?' Delight and suspicion jostled for supremacy. 'What for—kissing practice?'

He wavered only slightly. 'I'm working to a strict schedule, delivering chapter by chapter to my publisher. I haven't a hope of sticking to deadline unless I can find a typist.' He raised his bandaged hand with a gesture of helplessness. 'The other night you offered to help Michael if he needed the odd page re-done in a hurry. Would you consider typing for me, though it's more than just the odd page. We could kill two birds with one stone.'

'What do you mean?' Julia felt very thick. The kiss had shattered some of her illusions about big men, about Hugh in particular, and now she felt all at sea with him.

'I mean you come and type for me in the evenings. Let everyone draw their own conclusions about your visits.'

Left to herself Julia would have leapt at the idea, but she had to point out one very large stumbling block. 'Isn't it a bit out of character for you to fling your cap over the windmill with one of the hired helps? Highly unlikely, I would have thought. And might not Richard and Steve still . . .'

'I think you can safely leave the twins to me, Julia. They won't presume to trespass.'

When he spoke in that tone of voice Julia didn't presume to doubt his success. But she hesitated, disconcerted by the surge of pleasure she had felt when he had said he needed her. Needed, not *wanted*. His eyes were steady and unreadable and some of her pleasure faded. Still, he *had* asked her, even if it did seem as if it was against his better judgment . . .

'I'll pay you of course,' he added on, with casual cunning, as the silence lengthened, and Julia reared up, offended.

'You will not! I'll do it for free or not at all!' She stopped when she saw his satisfaction, realising she had played straight into his hands. 'You . . . you . . .'

Hugh undermined her indignation by getting up, drawing her attention to his injured hand in the process, reviving all her passionate guilt feelings.

'Oh well, I suppose it's worth a go,' she sighed, following him out of the pool. 'When do we start?'

'As soon as possible. Tonight. I'll take you out to dinner.'

'Out!' squeaked Julia, trotting, shivering, up the beach after him. 'I can't just go swanning off . . .'

'You're due an evening off—I checked with Connie. Don't look so outraged, Julia, nobody's going to starve—the girls are quite passable cooks when they try. Come on, you're going blue with cold. Pick up your things and let's get down to the changing sheds.'

'Yes, sir, Mr Fix-it, sir,' saluted Julia with a grin. He sounded so confident. But he needn't think he could order her around so casually all the time. No. She, Julia, was a human being, a woman, and she wasn't going to let him forget it. Especially now that she knew how exquisitely he kissed!

CHAPTER SEVEN

JULIA sighed as she screwed up and discarded another hand-written foolscap page. Her fingers ached from the intensive exercise. At first glance Hugh's IBM golfball self-correcting machine had seemed terrifying, a sleek, fearsome monster baring its keys like rows of gleaming teeth at her. Surprisingly, though, it had proved easy to use . . . so far.

Julia looked over to where Hugh sat in his brown leather wing-chair, grey head bent over his papers. The music of one of Bach's Brandenburg Concertos ebbed and flowed around them, absorbing the silence with its beauty. The lovely room made Julia appreciate why Hugh spent so much time up here. Long and rectangular, in the past it had been divided up into servants' quarters. When the renovations had been done, the timber from the walls had been re-cycled into a small bathroom and tiny kitchenette, and an extra dormer window added, bringing the number to three. Now it was a room to suit a large man and furnished in comfort, if not luxury. Travelling spotlights were attached to the heavily oiled kauri rafters, throwing warm pools of yellow on to the large desk where Julia sat, the leather suite which surrounded the large brick fireplace, and picking out the rich highlights in the beautiful Persian carpets which covered the polished floorboards.

At the far end of the room, in semi-darkness, was an enormous, ornately carved four-poster bed with feather mattress, down pillows and plain brown duvet. How Julia envied Hugh that bed! Whenever she took a break from the typewriter she would throw herself into the feather depths under Hugh's faintly amused gaze and relax in blissful pleasure.

Julia smiled to herself as her eyes wandered back to Hugh in his chair. In a way the bed was rather like its owner—large, dominating everything around it, yet on further exploration unexpectedly soft and warm. Julia had been working for him for three nights now and was aware that slowly, slowly, he was lowering his guard. No longer was she being treated with wary distaste, as a small, potentially explosive package. She was being useful, and at the same time showing him a quieter, calmer side of her personality.

The night they had gone out to dinner (leaving a house full of mouths agape behind) their conversation had pointed up their differences. Julia was a rock fan, Hugh preferred the classics: Julia was comedy and corny old movies, Hugh was a realist; Julia read widely and indiscriminately, Hugh was strictly non-fiction; Julia was a free-thinking liberal, Hugh a conservative. Still, she had enjoyed his company immensely, finding their differences stimulating, admiring his sophistication and maturity. They had talked about anything and everything, Julia matching Hugh's logical persuasiveness with her own fierce enthusiasm so that the conversational honours were more or less evenly divided.

Most importantly, their plan had been working. So understated were Hugh's emotions usually that he had achieved a dramatic effect by merely appearing to *notice* Julia. A glance, a light touch, a slight smile . . . to his family these seemed the equivalent of passionate embraces. Julia was vaguely disappointed that her role was so minor . . . and that there didn't seem the need for even an occasional kiss. She remembered the taste and feel of him that day on the beach, and how much she had liked it. She sighed heavily. Hugh hadn't lowered his guard that far . . . yet.

'Are you hinting that you've done enough for the evening?' She found herself being observed under lowered brows.

'Well, it is eleven, but I haven't finished the rest of chapter six yet,' she said, over a yawn.

The large grey head moved as he shrugged his shoulders with an unintelligible grunt.

'I'm a cook, not a typist,' grumbled Julia, interpreting his impatient rumble. She stood up and wandered over to the chair. When Hugh didn't look up she subsided on to the rug at his feet, moving her tired neck muscles as the fierce, dry heat of the fire soaked into her back. 'What are you doing?'

'Revision.' The gold pen continued to move smoothly across a typed page. Typed? Julia raised herself to peep over into his lap.

'Hey! That's the stuff I did yesterday. What's the point of my finishing chapter six if I have to start all over again?'

'I changed my mind about one or two things.'

Julia sat back again, wrapping her arms around her drawn-up knees, bunching her skirt modestly around her thighs as she looked at him in affectionate exasperation. 'You're such a perfectionist,' she complained. 'I don't think that anyone can meet your demands, not even yourself. At this rate you could go on revising forever.'

'The pursuit of perfection is what the law is all about.'

'If laws were perfect we wouldn't need lawyers to interpret the gobbledygook for the rest of us,' said Julia provokingly. She loved to tease him when he was so intense and serious, to draw him out. She knew his face well enough by now to judge the imperceptible signs of strain as they appeared after a long day absorbed in his work. Left to himself he would work all night, and be up again at dawn the next day. 'That would be you out of work for a start,' she added, after getting no response.

'I said the pursuit of,' replied Hugh, calmly crossing a T. He looked up and found her dancing eyes upon him. After a moment's hesitation he put down his pen, knowing full well what she was doing but ready to go along with it . . . for her sake, he told himself.

Julia rested her chin on one raised knee as he elaborated. When all else failed, casting slurs on his beloved law would always get him talking. He was a marvellously fluent speaker in his chosen subject and his soft, sonorous voice sounded a lovely counterpoint to Bach. Such a beautiful voice, thought Julia, closing her eyes and letting his words wash over her, how I love to hear him speak.

'You must be a very impressive lecturer,' she opened her eyes and smiled lazily at him when he finally flowed to a halt. 'I'm not surprised that Connie calls you the heart-throb of the Law Faculty.'

The broad, intelligent forehead creased with disapproval. 'Do you ever use that mind of yours to its full potential?' he asked with a hint of weariness. 'Don't you take anything seriously?'

Julia sat up straight. 'And don't you recognise a compliment when you hear one, even if it is an oblique one?' She would hate to slide back again in his estimation, to that of a frothy-minded idiot. 'I listened, I understood—most of it anyway. But I don't have the depth of knowledge to comment with any authority on the points you made. I have opinions, sure, but they're uninformed, as yet.' She didn't want to tell him that she had actually borrowed one of his books—*A Layman's Approach to New Zealand Law*—in an attempt to discover something of the fascination that his profession held for him. 'Anyway—I'm serious about lots of things.'

'For example?' Dry scepticism.

'My job. I'm very good at it and I want to be better. Cooking is a science as well as an art, it requires discipline and knowledge as well as flair. I admit that sometimes I have problems—after all, I'm not a naturally controlled personality . . .' she ignored his half laugh, 'but in the kitchen I have to subordinate myself to the job. That's partly why I like to let myself go outside it. I love cooking, but it can be tough—long hours and hard physical labour, especially restaurant work. I've studied and worked for years to get where I am today, I reckon I'm entitled to enjoy myself. Can't you accept that I like to laugh when I can because there are too many reasons in this cruel and unfair world to cry!'

'Oh, I can accept that,' said Hugh quietly, with an emphasis that told her he was about to say something that was very important to their relationship. 'What I have difficulty in coming to terms with is that often your humour seems directed at me . . . at what *I* take seriously.'

Julia was aghast that he should think she had so little respect for him, and secretly amazed that he should reveal such an insecurity. Did it really matter to him what she thought? Oh, please let it be so.

'That doesn't mean I don't care!' she cried, twisting to reach up and lay a small, reassuring hand on the hard knee beside her. 'Quite the reverse. I admire you tremendously for what you do, for the scope of your intelligence and your dedication—more than I can say. That's *why* I can tease you so freely. I only tease people I like . . . and you're such an irresistibly large target. You like it too; deep down, inside, you *smile*.'

'You know me so well?' he murmured quellingly.

'No, but I'm beginning to! Shall I come after lunch tomorrow and catch up on chapter six? I'd rather be up here working than slinking around down there trying to avoid the Inquisition.'

'I thought the situation was much improved.' Hugh leant back in the big chair and Julia felt the strong flex of muscle under her hand as he straightened his legs out in front of him. She was tempted to leave her hand where it was, but suddenly she was aware of the flesh under the cloth, of how much she wanted to run her fingers up that warm, hard thigh. Seated at his feet she had a foreshortened view of his powerful body. His head was tilted back, face half-masked by the shadow thrown by the flickering firelight against the wing of the chair, the spotlight reflecting off the white sheets on his lap.

'Richard and Steve aren't at each other's throats so much anymore, if that's what you mean,' said Julia, removing her hand reluctantly. 'They're on my back instead! It's all right for you, tucked away up here. I'm the one who has to face all that avid curiosity. I'm such a terrible liar, I always forget what I'm supposed to have admitted to.'

'You'll cope,' came the callous reply. 'But certainly, you can come up and work if you wish, as long as I know in advance.'

'Poor Hugh, how you hate company,' Julia mocked, thinking how lovely it would be to be able to drop in on him anytime, without an appointment, just to talk, or to watch him work.

'But yours is very necessary,' he said, unflatteringly honest, and they looked for a moment at his hand, the deep purple bruising on the fingers now beginning to edge into yellow. 'I'm sorry if you find it a bore.'

'A bore!' If only he knew! 'Hugh, don't be silly. Even if I find the text a bit heavy going, knowing *you* wrote it makes it interesting. You love it, don't you?'

'I find it rewarding and stimulating, yes.' How carefully he avoided the implications of that little word.

'Oh poof,' scoffed Julia. 'Don't be so wretchedly cautious! It's like me and cooking, a love affair. You know, Richard once told me that you chose your career because you didn't want to get involved in the untidy humanness of criminal law, but I don't think that's true. I think you followed your vocation. When you talk about books, your work, you come alive. If that's not love I don't know what is.'

'I must remember to be more careful. I didn't realise I was so transparent.'

'What's so terrible about that?'

'A good lawyer is like a good poker player. He never reveals his hand in his face.'

'If you were less poker-faced life might be a bit easier for me downstairs.' Julia gave a mock-sigh.

'In what way?' He sounded lazily interested, eyes screened by thick lashes as he looked down at her. Bach had come to an end some time ago and there was a faint buzz from the stereo speakers. Usually Hugh's tidy mind would have prompted him to turn it off by now, but tonight he seemed disinclined to move.

'What on earth do I see in you? You're too aloof for the likes of me. You're going to corrupt my innocent youth with your cold-blooded sophistication. You're too old and staid for me. And . . .' Richard had been very particular on this point, 'you can't give me the kind of loving I need.'

'I presume you had an answer for all that.'

'Oh yes,' Julia lowered her eyes demurely. 'I told them that you were the most fantastic kisser I'd ever met. That I'd never be able to settle for second-rate lips again. That you left them in the shade when it came to sending shivers up my spine.' She looked up. Hugh was laughing soundlessly and she wished she could freeze the image forever. She loved to make him laugh. 'Well, it's true, you do. It shut Richard up anyhow, no more remarks about you being old enough to be my father.'

'Hardly. And I might argue the case on one or two other of his allegations. How he got the impression that your innocence is a point at issue is beyond me.'

Julia laughed, not at what he said but at the way he said it. It had taken her a while but she was beginning to appreciate his dry, ironic sense of humour. And she couldn't blame him for what he thought—that she was as free and easy with her favours as she was with her words. She wondered at her own reluctance to enlighten him, sensing that it had its roots in the growing attraction she felt towards him. Hugh would run a mile from a virgin . . . too much of an emotional risk . . . but an experienced woman he might be prepared to meet on equal ground.

A log fell in the fire, sending out a shower of tea-tree sparks and Julia jumped, startled out of the beginnings of an erotic fantasy. She stood up and stretched, trying to shake off her sensual lethargy. Hugh watched the ripple of tension run through the curving arch of her body, breathing in a drift of the warm, earthy fragrance of the perfume she wore, and stood up, too.

Julia was heart-crashingly aware of the living, breathing man . . . so big, so strong, so close, and of her own nervous reaction to his nearness.

'Oh goodness, look at the time,' she babbled, looking at the grandfather clock by the door. 'I'd better go down and get supper for everyone.'

She scuttled to the door, barely hearing Hugh's 'good night', so anxious was she to get away before she did something stupid, like throw herself at him.

She had put the water on to boil and was sliding halved muffins under the grill of the gas cooker when Connie entered the kitchen, the girls at her heels.

'I was going to do that, Julia, I thought you were still upstairs.' There was no hint of condemnation in the words. 'Is Hugh coming down?'

Julia regarded her fondly. Since Hugh never came down for supper, the remark was in the nature of a gentle probe.

'No, he's . . .' she just stopped herself from saying *still working*, '. . . he's going to do some more work on his book.'

'How's it coming along?'

'Slowly, I think,' said Julia, thinking of the re-typing she would have to do tomorrow.

'Good.' Connie saw the three girls exchange surprised looks. 'I mean that it's good that he's not overdoing it. Hugh always did work too hard—making up, I guess. He needs a bit of creative diversion.'

'You can't get more creatively diverting than Julia,' said Ros with a sly wink.

'Don't let the children embarrass you, Julia darling,' Connie ordered imperiously. 'If you can encourage Hugh to relax and open up I shall be eternally grateful.

I expect you've discovered for yourself that under that crust he's a very strongly passionate man. What do you think of the four-poster?'

On the surface it was a change of subject, but Olivia evidently didn't think so: 'Mother!'

'What?' Connie made innocent eyes at her daughters. 'You don't think I was ...? Olivia, what a mind you have! Julia didn't think that, did you darling?'

'Not for a moment,' grinned Julia. The twins liked to consider themselves as sophisticated and every now and then Connie took it into her head to disabuse them. 'I think the bed is fantastic.'

'Hugh found it in some deceased estate sale in Thames. He doesn't usually put himself out for the sake of a possession. His Auckland flat's like a motel room. But something about that bed really struck a responsive chord.' Julia knew exactly what she meant ... it had struck the same chord with her. 'Are those muffins burning, Julia, or are they supposed to smoke like that!'

Three pairs of hands hurriedly helped to rescue the slightly singed muffins ('lovely and crisp, just how I like them,' consoled Ros). Julia slapped on the butter, silently admonishing herself. The merest mention of Hugh was turning into an occupational hazard; she must try to curb this obsessive curiosity.

'You'd better watch yourself though,' Connie continued without pause, 'I understand that thirteen children were conceived within those four posts ... a very *fertile* breeding ground for love, that bed.'

'Isn't she awful!' giggled Olivia as her mother swept out of the door. 'I mean, you have to admire her instinct for scene stealing, not to mention her breath control, but she does come out with the most *terrible* things.'

'Aren't all women supposed to become like their mothers?' Julia grinned, desperately trying to control her blush.

'I hope so!' Ros put bowls of jam and honey on the tray beside the plate of muffins. 'That puts me in line to be

the next doyenne of the New Zealand stage. Oh . . . I'll
miss her when I'm in England. I'll miss everyone. I'll be
rottenly homesick. How about changing your mind and
coming with me, Liv?'

'I told you, I haven't got the cash. We're not due our
Trust money until we're twenty-five,' Olivia explained
to Julia's surprised look. 'Meantime the parents have
this thing about us making it under our own steam
financially. Good for us, really.'

'If you went back to commercial art for a while it
wouldn't take you long to save the fare. And think of the
long-term benefits of going overseas,' insisted Ros,
pouring the tea while Julia dealt with the coffees.

'Logan says . . .'

'Oh, forget it,' Ros interrupted impatiently. 'It was a
stupid idea anyway. I'll take this tea through for you,
Julia.'

Olivia looked after her sister. 'I can't just walk out on
Logan and the others . . . not with this exhibition coming
up.'

Can't you? wondered Julia, detecting a certain
wistfulness in the pale oval face. Maybe Olivia *wanted*
a nudge towards 'walking out', an excuse to break
away.

In the lounge Julia took up her favourite supper
position on the floor by the brass coal scuttle, sipping
her tea as she watched the family chatter about its day.
She raised a weak smile when Steve stepped over
Charley, sprawling on the floor studying a *Mechanics*
magazine, and sat beside her.

'I finished my song this morning. Would you like to
hear it sometime tomorrow?'

'I'm not sure when,' Julia prevaricated. 'I'll be up
with Hugh in the morning.'

'I only want you to listen, truly,' he said quietly. 'It's
good, Julia, really good . . . a whole new kind of song
for me. Look . . .' he cast a brief look at Richard,
brooding half-heartedly in the corner of the room, '. . . I

know I was a little crazy for a while there, but I've got my head together now. No more heavy stuff, OK?'

'OK,' Julia was relieved, but still careful. She lowered her voice. 'And you're all right now, about the other?'

The green eyes were clear and sharp. 'Wait until you hear *Julia*, then you'll *know*. I've still got the music in me, *with* me. And I put my foot down with Zak . . . no more work until I'm ready.' He smiled then, one of Richard's charming smiles, and Julia immediately smelt collaboration. 'Tell me . . . are you and Hugh, really, you know . . . have you really got something going, or was that all just for our benefit?'

Julia opened her mouth to utter the white lie, and to her astonishment found herself telling the truth: 'No it's not for your benefit, it's for mine. He's the most fascinating man I've ever met. I l-like him very, very much.'

Her blush as much as that revealing stumble seemed to convince Steve. 'I'm glad,' he said, and she could see that he was. Why hadn't she gone ahead and said 'love'? it wouldn't have been a lie either. She did love him, impossible as it seemed—all those much-discussed signs were there: extreme self-awareness in his presence, the shortness of breath, the tingling, the constant desire to touch him both mentally and physically. When had liking 'very, very much' turned into loving? She didn't know. Nor did she know very much about Hugh's feelings. He was attracted to her, she could sense that, but he was reluctant to pursue it, she sensed that, too. They were both aware of their extreme personality differences—perhaps, for Hugh, that was the deciding factor. He wasn't one to be carried away by his emotions, or his passions, everything was tightly controlled by his intelligence. Julia on the other hand was willing to ride with her instincts. This newly discovered love was a heady experience to be explored, a kind of natural high. Was this how Steve had felt when pumped full of his drugs? If so, Julia could appreciate the attraction of maintaining the state indefinitely. She could only hope that her addiction didn't end as miserably as Steve's, but she refused to dwell on all the negative possibilities, there were too many of them. For now she would make the most of it, enjoy the next few days in Hugh's company, and do all she could to nurture the attraction.

To this end she offered, the next morning, to type for him in the afternoon as well. To her chagrin, though Hugh accepted the offer, he went on to tell her that he would be spending the afternoon in Whitianga. She typed disconsolately for half an hour in his absence, wishing she hadn't been in such a hurry to get away from Steve. His song, *Julia* had turned out to be a hauntingly catchy ballad of love, not the tale of hard-hearted betrayal she had feared it might have turned into!

Julia frowned at the lines of type fading across the page. That ribbon *had* to be changed. Recklessly, she decided to tackle it herself ... perhaps the jinx would be merciful.

'Oh God, what have I done?' A few minutes later Julia surveyed the mess in horror. How had the cartridge got jammed like that? She poked at it with a ballpoint and somehow a foot of ribbon spat out at her. The more she fiddled, the worse the snarl became and Julia managed to cover the typewriter, herself, and several pages of typescript with inky fingerprints whilst trying to cram everything back. Long, sweaty minutes passed, then the grandfather clock struck doom.

'Oh God!'

Time to go down and prepare the marinade for the satay. Tonight was supposed to be a double celebration—Steve's new song and Michael's completed play. She turned her back on the sneering typewriter and fled, vowing to be back before Hugh.

She scrubbed her hands in the kitchen sink, expertly cut up the two plump, fresh chickens with a razor-sharp cleaver and put the pieces into a glass dish. Handfuls of chillis, ginger-root, and onion were thrown into the blender, followed up with generous slurps of soy sauce, oil and water (so much for the precise science of cooking!). One loud and angry whizz, and whip off the lid to push down the ingredients with her rubber spatula . . .

'Something smells interesting.'

'Waahhh!' Julia's hand slipped and punched the blender's control button. The thick, oily, sludge exploded with a roar out of the open top, splattering reddish blobs all over the kitchen, including the frozen figures of Julia and Hugh. Some of them even reached the eight-foot ceiling.

'Turn that bloody thing off!' yelled Hugh over the racket, lurching forward to slam his hand down on the button, switching the grinding mechanism off. 'Damn you to hell, Julia, I thought you said you never had accidents in the kitchen!'

Some of the marinade had flown into Julia's horrified open mouth and she coughed furiously to rid herself of the peppery heat. When the tears cleared from her eyes and she saw Hugh's livid expression her gaze skittered down his suit and lingered . . .

'Isn't that the suit . . .?' she croaked to a halt at his hissing, indrawn breath.

'The very same! Thanks to a good dry-cleaner it survived its dunking . . . but this time you can pay in full for your damned stupidity!'

She couldn't blame him, the suit was freckled all over with oily spots, and he had, after all, fronted up with the money for her car bill without argument. Poor Hugh, he was quite rigid with anger, wrinkling his nose at the potent smell enveloping them, dabbing at his face with a no-longer-spotless white handkerchief.

Julia began to giggle and the giggles grew. Soon she was leaning against the kitchen table helpless with laughter, fresh tears streaming down her face, stomach tortured by mirthful spasms.

'Oh, I'm sorry, I'm so sorry . . .' she hiccupped semi-hysterically. 'But you look . . . oh, Hugh, your poor dignity . . . you look as if you've got measles!'

'And I warned you once before about laughing at me,' said Hugh in a peculiarly goaded tone of voice.

He reached out a large hand and before Julia could move he had snatched her off her feet, hands almost completely spanning her waist. She was lifted high, dangling like a rag doll against his body, gasping with astonishment and clutching at his wrists to support herself upright. Her heart thundered at his expression. He was angry but his anger was tightly controlled, and Julia knew instinctively that he wouldn't use his superior strength to physically hurt her. If she struggled he would let her go.

'What are you going to do?' she asked breathlessly, with conscious challenge, knowing already what he was going to do, and wanting him to do it.

'Something I shouldn't,' he muttered, lowering her against his mouth, sending sparkling streaks of exhilaration through her body as his limber tongue invaded her mouth, punishing with pleasure. He held her easily, as if she weighed nothing, as he kissed her, tilting and turning her small body with his hands so that he could explore her mouth from different angles. Julia's hands left the rigid tendons of his wrists and clutched at the solid warmth of his neck as she felt him move, carrying her backwards, hard thighs bumping between her dangling legs.

He stopped and slowly, slowly, let her slide through his hard embrace until her toes touched the floor. From hip to shoulder Julia's body burned at the crushing, sliding friction down the length of the masculine torso. Now the long fingers angled firmly under her arms, thumbs pressing into the soft undersides of her breasts. Julia melted into him, sliding her arms under his jacket, around to his back where her hands spread across the hard-packed flesh, nails burrowing into the warmth, urging him closer. She was on her tip toes, head buzzing with pleasurable sensations, opening to him as his mouth clung hotly, drifted and clung again. It felt so good, even better than it had before.

'For a moment I thought you were going to put me over your knee,' she said dreamily as he nibbled the point of her chin, thumbs beginning a lazy movement which stroked the soft wool of her sweater against the ultra-sensitive skin of her breasts, making them tauten and sending a lick of heat plunging to her belly.

She felt him lean against her so that the hard edge of the kitchen table dug into her buttocks. Slowly, slowly he continued the lean until Julia was arched back, flat against the table top, oblivious to the pool of marinade soaking into the back of her sweater as she stared into the grey-blue eyes glittering into hers. Were they getting bluer, or was that just the reflection of her own, so close to his?

'I haven't finished with you yet,' he threatened softly, adding huskily: 'I get the feeling that you wouldn't object to anything I did to you . . . and there's so much I could do.' He buried his mouth in hers again, this time with a questing urgency which startled and excited Julia, making her forget as completely as he obviously had how vulnerable they were to interruption.

The broad chest hovered over her as she felt his hands leave her then gasped as she felt them slide smoothly up under her loose sweater, silking over the lycra leotard she was wearing for warmth, splaying heavily out over her generous breasts. Julia shuddered against him, her back arching further as the cupping, massaging motion of his fingers took effect. She groaned his name, glad she had worn no bra, glad that she fitted so perfectly into his hands. She had never felt such an urgent need for assuagement, a need which overrode inhibition and common sense, and stripped away all her preconceptions of what naked passion could be. His fingers were soft, subtle, skilful, bringing her nipples to burgeoning fullness through the thin lycra, teasing out her response so that Julia bloomed with the rising of her blood.

Her legs, hanging over the side of the table, were trapped by the crowding strength of his and Julia twitched them helplessly, aching to wrap them licentiously around him, to draw him even closer than was physically possible.

His mouth lifted at her restless movement and he stared down at her hectically flushed face, still glistening under its light application of pink oil. He was breathing as hard as she was, but he brought it quickly under control, the massive chest expanding and contracting rhythmically, the only sign of colour on the tips of his ears. Julia watched dazedly as he licked his lips experimentally, his mouth reddened to sensual fullness by long contact with hers.

'You taste so hot and spicy. Kissing you is like eating fire.' He ducked and stroked his tongue over her jawbone, nudging her head around so that he could take the soft, fleshy lobe of her small ear into his mouth and suckle it with a firm, tugging pressure that was incredibly erotic. Julia sighed with pleasure, not wanting him to stop, and turned her head so that he could get access to the other ear. Her eyes fluttered open, blurring slightly, then focusing sharply on the interested face of Charley, peeping around the open back door!

CHAPTER EIGHT

JULIA gave a strangled squawk and heaved with all her might at the rock-solid chest above her. Hugh didn't budge an inch, but he did look over his shoulder to see what had brought on her sudden protest. At the sight of Charley he made a brief murmur and straightened, sliding his hands out from under Julia's sweater witn unhurried ease.

'Did one of you explode?' Charley grinned, venturing on to the slippery kitchen floor. Oh yes, he was definitely growing up. Two years ago he would have melted in embarrassment, but now it was Julia who blushed, rolling off the table and yanking at her suggestively rumpled sweater.

'An accident with my blender,' Julia managed huskily, thrusting a tangle of curls off her hot brow.

'Oh. Are you OK?' Charley knew all about her jinx.

'I wasn't kissing her for medical reasons, Charley, if that's what's worrying you,' Hugh cut in smoothly. Julia sent him a speaking look. He sounded quite unruffled, yet a few moments ago he had been practically raping her on the kitchen table. Well, not raping exactly ... whatever the definition, he had no right to behave with such calm when Julia was still flushed and aroused, her heart pounding fit to burst.

'Were you looking for me?' she asked Charley, trying to get a grip on reality.

He was. He wanted to take the VW for a test run, and not having obtained his drivers' licence yet, he wanted Julia to drive him. To her surprise Hugh stepped in again, this time to offer his services as chauffeur while Julia cleaned up the kitchen. Charley appeared so pleased Julia didn't have the heart to argue, but she couldn't help feeling somewhat put out as the two males wandered out in companionable conversation, ignoring her pique.

So frantic was she for the rest of the evening, salvaging her chicken recipe, that Julia quite forgot about Hugh's typewriter. It wasn't until she joined the others in the lounge for pre-dinner drinks and saw Hugh attired in yet another immaculate suit that she remembered. Hell!

Accepting a sherry from Michael, Julia felt a niggle of disquiet as she saw that Hugh was holding one too. He wasn't the teetotaller she had thought, she had discovered that when they went out to dinner together, but he drank only sparingly, and never when he had work to do. Did that—*gulp*—mean that his typewriter was still out of action? Julia sneaked a look at his face. As usual unreadable, though the grey eyes were narrowed on her in a most unsettling way. She flashed him a quick, nervous smile, then regretted it when he began to move across the room towards her.

'What a lovely dress, Julia,' she heard Olivia beside her exclaim. In honour of the occasion Julia had put on the only long dress she had brought with her—a pure-silk butterfly dress. 'It's hand-painted isn't it? What a fabulous design. Where did you get it?'

'Umm, in Auckland,' said Julia distractedly as Hugh joined their little group. 'Browns Mill actually, you know, the craft place. The designer specialises in unique, hand-painted silks.'

'As unique and as beautiful as the woman who's wearing it,' Richard chipped in lavishly. 'Ah ... *"she hangs upon the cheek of the night like a rich jewel in an Ethiop's ear"*.'

'Your Herrick put it far more aptly, I think, Richard.' Julia held her breath at Hugh's quiet interjection. Avoiding his gaze her eyes sank to the injured hand holding his glass. There was a faint, dark smudge on his wrist. Ink? Oh dear ... Nervously she

watched his other hand reach out to catch one of the
fluttering points of her sleeve, pulling it so that she had
to turn to fully face him. She didn't know quite what
she was expecting, but his first, soft words had her eyes
rearing, startled, to his.

> ' "When as in silks my *Julia* goes,
> Then, then (*me thinks*) how sweetly flowes
> That liquifaction of her clothes.
> Next, when I cast mine eyes and see
> That brave vibration each way free;
> O how that glittering taketh me!" '

Julia was mesmerised, as much by the indecently
honeyed tone of his voice as by the way his grey eyes
slid over her face, over the silk to where it drew taut
across her breasts, reminding them both of how he had
touched them. Indeed they began to ache, as if he was
touching them now.

'Oh, very appropriate,' sniped Richard sourly.
'Poetry, yet, big brother. You'll be taking to the boards
next.'

'The kind of poetry that suits Julia is rather
unsuitable for public performance,' returned Hugh
smoothly, not taking his eyes off a blushing Julia.

All through dinner it was the same, Hugh topping
every endeavour of Richard's to gain Julia's attention.
After she got over her initial breathless confusion Julia
was tongue-tied by a mixture of embarrassment and
annoyance at his heavy-handedness. He was being so
obvious, surely everyone knew he was being sarcastic?
But Connie was beaming benignly at them, Charley
grinning knowingly and the others richly entertained by
the romantic contest. Only for Julia was it a penance,
knowing it was Hugh's way of getting back at her.

'Will you cut it out, you're making everyone
suspicious,' she hissed desperately at Hugh as he leapt
to pull out her chair when they all rose to leave the
table.

'Nonsense, they're loving it,' he murmured blandly into her ear. Catching Ros's lascivious wink Julia knew he spoke the truth. 'And look at Richard ... on his last legs. If I can be moved to such revolting sentimentality he knows he may as well throw in the towel.'

Julia clenched her fists to stop herself throttling him. Revolting sentimentality! It was beautiful, heart-stopping ... if only it was sincere. Oh, how she longed for him to mean every single sentimental word of his wooing. It gave her the shivers, imagining what it would be like to have Hugh so completely and utterly in love with her that he laid his heart at her feet with delicious phrases ... *O how that glittering taketh me!* She escaped from her hut flushes into the kitchen, where she put the coffee on. Drifting back into the hall, wrapped in cosy dreams of mutual and everlasting love, she ran into Richard as he came out of the dining room. He struck a dramatic pose of woe.

' "*Farewell, farewell, one kiss and I'll descend.*" '

'Ohh, Richard, not now!' snapped Julia.

'Dear Juliet, why art thou yet so fair?' He grinned at her fierce scowl. 'You can take that hideous expression off your face, love. I concede.'

Julia viewed his graceful gesture with suspicion.

'You know what Byron said about friendship?' he continued with rueful charm. 'It's love without his wings.'

'Well, we are kiwis,' murmured Julia, naming New Zealand's unique flightless native bird. Her heart sank into her shoes. The last thing she wanted to do was to call off the charade with Hugh. She wanted more time, *needed* more time, to show him that their relationship was worth something for its own sake.

'*I* am,' said Richard. 'I'm beginning to think that you and Hugh are birds of a different feather.'

'Are you two coming? Or are you going to stand out there exchanging clichés all night?' It was Hugh, standing in the lounge doorway. 'We're going to toast Steve and Michael with the rest of the champagne.'

He reached out a casual arm and hauled Julia against him as she walked past, anchoring her there so that she was forced to share his glass of champagne. How much had he heard? Probably too much for her to pretend that Richard was still going to be a problem. And weren't they all drinking to Steve's recovery? She felt torn in two, and Hugh's mockery suddenly became too much to stand.

'If you don't mind, I think I'll have an early night,' she told the assembled gathering after coffee had been distributed.

'Good idea.' Hugh put his own cup down.

'Go ahead,' said Michael drily. 'Why should the night of my triumph over the Muse be different from any other night?'

'Don't be a sourpuss, darling,' scolded his wife. 'You two go on up,' she said to Julia and Hugh, for all the world as if they were an old married couple. 'The twins can help if I need assistance to wheel the old man away. He always gets stonkered when he finishes a play. Not a pretty sight.'

'We could stay a little longer ...' offered Hugh, but Julia, sick of playacting, leapt in with both feet.

'No we can't,' she said flatly, and flushed as everyone looked at her, tucked within the circle of Hugh's arm.

'That's OK, we understand,' Ros grinned at her eagerness. 'Just remember what Connie told you about the you-know-what.'

Hugh raised an eyebrow and Julia gave a tiny groan as she dragged him upstairs and rounded on him fiercely.

'You're worse than Richard, you know that!' she accused distractedly. 'You made them think ... them think ...' She stuttered to a stop in the face of his amusement. 'There was no need to be so ... so ...'

'Amorous?'

'Lecherous!' she howled, enraged by the smile that so usually enchanted her. He had no right to be so unfeeling.

'What's the matter, Julia?' he asked with soft emphasis. 'You can dish it out but you can't take it? Not so amusing when *you're* the butt of a joke, is it?'

So she had been correct in thinking he was teaching her a lesson. 'You . . . you . . .' How could she blurt out that to her it was no joke, that the lesson was more painful than he could possibly have conceived. For the first time in her life she had to control her instinct to tell the truth, holding back the words until she was almost bursting with the frustration of it.

'Now, Julia, don't lose your splendid sense of humour. You want me to be less solemn don't you? And still you're not happy.'

'What happened to your much-vaunted subtlety?' she cried weakly, backed into a corner by his inescapable logic. If she felt he had done it to gain her approval her spirits might have lifted, but that hadn't been his aim.

'You're not a subtle woman,' he pointed out gently. 'Perhaps you might now feel more sympathetic towards those who are less extrovert than yourself.'

Julia suddenly caught sight of his typewriter sitting, now innocent of stain, on an extremely tidy desk. She grabbed the chance of a diversion. 'I meant to tell you about the typewriter, I really did. But I didn't do anything, Hugh, I was just trying to——'

'Please, spare me. Charley filled me in on your mechanical problems. Next time it happens, let me deal with it.'

'Yes, Hugh,' she said humbly. At least there *was* going to be a next time, by the sound of it, he wasn't going to cast her aside immediately. The reprieve made her bolder. 'He wants to be a mechanic, did he tell you?'

A wary expression cooled Hugh's eyes. 'Yes.'

'Well?'

'Well what?'

'What are you going to do about it?'

'Me?'

'Yes, you.' This was a Hugh she was very familiar

with. 'You're his big brother. You're a lawyer, you could present a good case to Michael and Connie, prepare the way so to speak. You told me yourself he'd done an excellent job on my car.' He had made it seem like another of his whispered sweet nothings at the dinner table.

'I'll see.' Hugh moved away from her but Julia followed.

'What will you see?'

'I'll see what I can do.' His tone brooked no argument and Julia, still unsatisfied, pursued another line.

'While you're about it, there's Olivia.'

Hugh lifted his head wearily. 'What a receptive bosom you have, Julia.'

His sarcasm hurt. 'There's no need to sneer, just because *you* don't use my bosom to cry on.'

'If I use your breasts at all, Julia, it won't be for crying on,' he said softly, in wry self-derision, his eyes flickering down.

The blood drummed in Julia's head as she stared at him, her mouth slightly open. She felt instantly hot, her breathing all out of control. Did he know what that sort of comment did to her? Of course he did, he must. She stirred uneasily under his veiled gaze. What was he thinking? And was it as erotic as what she had in mind? No, he was just trying to distract her train of thought . . . as she had done earlier to him with her comment about the typewriter.

'Yes, um, well . . . about Olivia.' Her voice came out in an embarrassing croak which smoothed out as she explained the situation.

'How you love to interfere in other people's lives, Julia. Fortunately I have no such compulsion.'

'Giving someone a viable alternative isn't interfering,' she protested. 'She needs an escape clause from that commune, that's all.'

'It's nothing to do with me, leave me out of it.' Evenness edged into impatience.

'Oh yes it is. You've gone all lawyer-like. You always do that when you feel defensive.'

'Don't try me too far, Julia,' he said dangerously. 'Be satisfied with Charley. I know what you're trying to do and it won't work. I am not going to get involved.'

'But you are involved already,' she said triumphantly. 'Look how involved you were tonight—and look how much you enjoyed yourself. You did, you know!' as he opened his mouth. 'Even if *I* didn't, I could see that much. All right, all right, I'm going!' she held her hands up and backed away as the broad jaw firmed, sensing she would get no further. Obviously Hugh had no intention of working tonight, at least not with her. Much as she wanted to stay she sensed that Hugh had reached the limit of his patience. Perhaps he was even a little dismayed at his uncharacteristic behaviour.

Later she had reason to be glad that she had left quietly. That night proved to be another turning point in their relationship, the start of a mutual journey of discovery. Julia still laughed and teased, but with a loving sensitivity that held no sting, while Hugh in his turn guided her more willingly into his world. The reluctant fascination with which he watched her became less reluctant. No longer did it disturb him if a piece of music, selected specifically to educate her inexperienced ears to the complexities of the classical repertoire, prompted Julia to dance, swirling across the Persian carpets in uninhibited physical response to its. beauty. He would lie in his favourite chair, eyes half-closed as they followed her movements, content in the realisation that, though hers was still a sensual rather than intellectual appreciation of music, she had the capacity for both. He could even admit to himself that he was enjoying her slow process of discovery, the freshness of her outlook provoking him to re-appraise his own response to the music which was so familiar to him, so much of a refuge.

Neither of them mentioned Hugh's fast-healing hand,

quite capable by now of using a typewriter. By tacit agreement the pace of their work slowed, allowing more time for conversation. At last Julia felt that he was beginning to trust her, to know her. But knowing was a long way from loving. It was impossible to tell, from Hugh's controlled demeanour, what he was feeling, but the physical tension that hovered between them on occasion told her at least that he was aware of a certain attraction. Of course, a man like Hugh wouldn't fall in love with the ease of someone who was as emotionally secure as Julia. She wasn't even sure that he *had* the capacity for her kind of loving, the whole-hearted, generous kind; but if not, she would have enough for both of them. When Julia gave herself, it would be without reservation.

She found the experience of being in love rather strange, both a pain and a pleasure. Every now and then she would inspect the fledgeling emotion and wonder at its secret splendour, waiting, wondering how or when it would grow to maturity. How different love was from her girlish fantasies ... not a clap of thunder and a bright shining light, but a thing alive, growing, climbing, twining itself around her, each day sending out delicate new tendrils, soft yet incredibly strong. And more incredible still, that her love not be Phillip's 'Latin hysteric', but a big, thoughtful, slow-moving man who pondered each word before he spoke, whose attractiveness was inextricably bound up with his intelligence.

One evening, late enough that the attic room had grown uncomfortably hot from the fire, Julia drowsed on the couch like a sleepy kitten, watching Hugh as he unbuttoned the starched collar of his shirt and flexed his muscular shoulders.

'How did you get to be such a size?' She stretched with a yawn. 'Mrs B said you used to be a scrawny little thing.'

'So I was. A prime target for school bullies. I decided that I needed some size and weight to deter the taunts.'

'Boxing? Judo?' Julia guessed teasingly.

He looked down at his hands as he stood before her—large, strong hands. 'I don't believe in physical violence.'

'No smacking your children then?' she asked lightly, and was taken aback by the silver flame that darted from his eyes.

'The question is hypothetical.'

Did that mean he didn't want children or couldn't have them? Julia was disturbed. Whatever vague and impossible dreams she had had about herself and Hugh, children had been a natural part of them. Hadn't everyone said how gentle and kind he was with children? Maybe he meant he would never get married. Well, that was something she could live with . . . if there was no other choice.

'I took up body-building.' As if he had sensed her curiosity, Hugh drew her off with his next words.

Julia's eyes widened. 'You pumped iron? Like the Incredible Hulk?'

'If you mean like the man who played the part, yes.'

Julia laughed delightedly, and told him about her first impression of him, coming towards her from his car. 'Tell me, did you pose, and all that other macho stuff?'

'I didn't perform in competition, no. I concentrated on weight-lifting.'

Yes, Julia could imagine it. Hugh sweating it out alone in a gym, engaged in a grim, private battle with his own body, and winning.

'Show me,' she ordered, sitting up from her semi-reclining position.

'What?'

'Show me how your muscles work.'

'I told you, I didn't pose.' He looked down his nose at her but Julia could be as stubborn as he.

'Rubbish. I bet you did it in front of the mirror when nobody was about.'

'I haven't lifted a weight in eight months.'

'So what? You're still in great condition.' Julia jumped up from the couch and grabbed at the buttons on his shirt. 'Aw, come on Hugh, I've never seen a man flex his muscles in the flesh.'

'No, Julia . . .' Hugh clamped his hand over hers.

'Don't be shy, Hugh, I've seen you with more than just your shirt off, remember? Please.' The memory spurred her on, her sudden desire to see him as she had that day on the beach intensifying. She wriggled her hands out of his and pulled his shirt open, going up on tiptoe to try and push it over his wide shoulders. He resisted and there was an undignified tussle, which Hugh lost by virtue of the fact that her small, pale hands moving over his chest seemed to have a mesmerising effect on him. Julia tossed his shirt over her shoulder and laughed triumphantly up at him.

'Show me,' she urged, her voice made husky by the knowledge that she was asking for more than a mere display of his muscles. She was close enough to feel the heat from his body and it seemed to radiate a more scorching heat than the fire behind her.

Slowly Hugh obliged, stripped of humour and embarrassment by Julia's sultry-eyed fascination. The atmosphere became charged with expectancy as she watched the beautifully meshed workings of his magnificent body, drawn like a magnet to its silent, potent maleness.

He froze as she raised an oddly trembling hand to stroke lightly across his bulging pectorals. 'So smooth, so hard,' she murmured, 'like hardwood under velvet. You're quite the most beautiful man I've ever seen.' She felt so small and feminine, enravished by this intensely personal exhibition of rippling power.

His hand caught at hers, but instead of pushing her away he held it hard against the warm brush of his chest so that she could feel the steady, slightly fast, rhythmic pulse of his heart. Her own was skipping erratically and her lips parted on a sigh of welcome as she watched his tightly controlled mouth come closer and closer to hover just above hers.

'Usually-so-honest-Julia. Why so coy? This is what you want, isn't it?'

He didn't need to wait for a reply. Julia arched towards him and his arms went around her, binding her firmly to his broad chest, burying her body against his. His kiss was as devastating as ever and Julia responded greedily to its lure, kicking off her shoes and leaning into him as she felt his tongue seek out the rough-smooth, hard-soft interiors of her mouth.

'You're so tiny in my arms,' he groaned thickly against her lips. 'Like a baby, so fresh and sweet.'

'I don't feel in the least babyish,' she muttered feverishly, denying the self-reproach implicit in his words. She couldn't bear it if he drew back now, if he used his damnable logic to talk himself out of satisfying them both.

'Show me how grown up you are, then,' he ordered, the large hands dealing with the buttons of her blouse with extraordinary delicacy as he kissed her mouth, her eyes, her ears, her neck, the warm pulse in her collarbone as it throbbed her excitement.

'Oh no, most definitely not a baby.' His soft words sent the blood rushing to her head as he cupped the fullness of her unfettered breasts, aroused by their round ripeness and the way they nestled warmly in his palms. 'But still, I think it's time you were in bed.'

She felt the smooth slide of a muscular arm at the back of her knees and the swift shift of his body that tilted her off-balance to be hoisted high against his chest. This time he let her down, not on a hard, wet table, but in the feathery nest of warmth that was his bed. He came down too, engulfing her with his heated flesh, pressing her further into the softness.

'As Richard pointed out on one memorable occasion, I'm a little too old for love-making on the floor,' he

apologised with a dry humour that made Julia blink
sensuously at him, and tease:

'What does Richard know? I think you're in fantastic
condition. Maybe later we can go back and I can show
you how wrong you are ...'

'My God, if anyone could, you could,' he growled,
pulling off her blouse and fumbling for the zip of her
skirt.

'Well, you know what they say about younger
women ... we renew a man's virility,' Julia gurgled, full
to the brim with love and laughter, relishing her first
experience of teasing foreplay, both physical and verbal.
'Here, let me do that.'

With a lithe and natural sensuality she slipped out of
her skirt and peeled off her pantyhose and tiny bikini
briefs. She was shivering with anticipation, eager to
touch and be touched, and her eagerness banished
virginal reticence and further aroused the man who
watched her prepare herself to receive his body.

He kissed her, long and hard, as if he couldn't help it,
then drew back to study her nakedness with his
customary eye for detail: the white skin, even whiter
across her breasts and hips—the luscious rise of the
twin peaks and their hard, rosy crests, the rounded
kissing-curve of her belly with its faintest suggestion of
baby down, the tender blonde vee between the soft rise
of her thighs. He touched her, experimentally, and felt
her tauten, heard her aching sigh. A slight flush
mounted his cheekbones and the tips of his ears and
Julia reached up to stroke them, rejoicing in her
freedom to do so.

No man had ever looked on her thus and Julia
gloried that Hugh should be the first, that she could
bring such an expression of passionate desire to the
normally shuttered grey eyes. She wasn't afraid of what
was to come, she wanted it so; she didn't feel like a
virgin, she felt all woman, limbs heavy, languid, and she
had no intention of breaking the spell of sexual urgency

by revealing the truth of her inexperience. She would tell him later, if he did not realise it for himself. Men always knew, didn't they, or was that a myth about to be exploded?

His hand moved to tilt her head to the side. 'Let's make love,' he whispered softly and his eyes closed as he kissed her very, very gently. Only their mouths touched as they savoured the taste of mutual arousal, until Julia, able to bear it no longer, rolled on to her side and pressed her body against his, the tips of her breasts flowering against the silky tease of his chest and her thighs trembling as she felt the thrust of his long legs. His kiss changed from gentle to very adult, his tongue forcing her lips wider as his hands slid around her hips, fingers sinking into the dimpled globes of her buttocks, lifting her against him, fitting her tightly to the contours of his body.

She groaned at the excess of pleasure, head falling back against the mounded pillows as his mouth played with her ear-lobes, nipped softly at her throat. So this was love, this twisting, wrenching inner tension, this driving force that compelled her to writhe against the hard masculinity beside her. She felt the large hands move to her waist, holding her down on her back again as his mouth sought further and Julia cried out as his lips described lazy circles around her breasts. She caught the short, grey hair between her clutching fingers, holding his head as she arched herself against him.

'Please, Hugh . . .' she pleaded quiveringly, her brain losing its tenuous links with the world outside his arms.

'I intend to please both of us, little one,' he vowed huskily, his hands tightening as he controlled her eagerness even as he encouraged it. 'Watch me, Julia. Tell me how I please you.'

Julia's eyes fluttered as she obeyed, reaching a pitch of desire as she saw his head dip to her breast, his lips part as he slowly, sensuously curled his moist tongue around an erect nipple, drawing it up into his open mouth. One hand moved up to cup the weight of her breast, lifting its fullness so that he could absorb more of the puckered pink into the scalding interior of his mouth. He was making soft sounds of enjoyment against her flesh and Julia closed her eyes again, dizzied by the image of his grey head moving against her body. Wave after wave of pure, unadulterated sensation hit her; the musky scent of him filled her nostrils, the slither of skin and soft rustle of the bed beneath them stole into her ears. Her legs moved involuntarily and he threw one of his across them, pinning her down while his hands made tiny, stroking motions across her stomach. He was touching her as if she was a tiny, precious, breakable object to be minutely explored.

In turn Julia explored him, her fingers delighting in what they found. His smooth, taut skin was faintly damp and alive with tension. Julia could feel the drawing in of his muscles as her hands stroked down to his hips where they lingered helplessly, wanting to seek his nakedness but hampered by inexperience.

His mouth left her breasts and trailed down to her stomach, then rimmed the bowl of her hips. Gasping, Julia pulled his head away, her fingers clenched in his hair, staring at him with a breathless intermingling of shock and excitement.

He met her wide-eyed gaze with puzzlement, then looked down at himself, misinterpreting her shyness.

'You're right. I'm over-dressed.' He sounded as if he had just succeeded in lifting a personal best . . . his voice harshened by adrenalin surging through his body, muscles responding fluidly as he swung off the bed and quickly stripped off the rest of his clothing.

'Better?' he murmured and Julia felt the sag of the bed as he re-joined her. She had not dared look but she gave a choking cry as he pulled her hands against him and she felt his hard nakedness. His sigh of satisfaction, the sudden shudder of his body changed the moment of fearful discovery into one of wonderment. It felt so searingly sweet, so meltingly, achingly, good to hold him like this. The very essence of his manhood was held in her small, trembling hands. It was she who made him like this; she whom he wanted so much that he had abandoned his protective persona.

'You're so big,' she murmured faintly, the pulse points of her body throbbing with congestion as he gently straddled her, careful not to lean his full weight on her, careful that she should feel all pleasure and no pain.

'You're always saying that to me,' he muttered thickly, with the remnant of their earlier teasing, 'but this time I'm flattered.' Aroused as he was, he was still sufficiently in control to reassure the age-old woman's fear: 'I won't hurt you, Julia. I'll wait until you're ready. Your smallness will make it good for both of us.'

She couldn't speak, everything roughly shouldered aside by the growing urgency of her passion, the gentle skill of his fingers, the conviction that this was the one man who had the right to take her virginity, to accept her love.

She felt him ease one powerful, thickly-haired thigh between hers to nudge them apart, felt his chest skim hers as he supported himself on tautly strained arms on either side of her head. His body, that magnificent structure of sensuous pleasure, seemed to crush all sensation into one place, everything focused on the hardness settling between her legs. Involuntarily, the words came:

'Oh, Hugh, I love you ... love me, please.' She repeated the litany mindlessly, consumed with anticipation.

'You mean, you want me,' he corrected her absently as he sought her softness.

'I love you,' she said again and this time she registered a slight stiffening of his body.

'You don't mean that, Julia,' he muttered, struggling

to hold back, body tense with the effort. 'We don't need love-lies. Let's enjoy this for what it is.'

'Do you think I'd be here like this if I didn't love you?' Julia moaned through kiss-stung lips, wanting to give herself to him, body and soul, in consummation.

He raised his head, body still as death. 'Frankly, yes,' he stated brutally looking down at their bodies so nearly conjoined, seeing the passion-swollen breasts, the small white hips covered by the broad saddle of his. 'I want your body, Julia—and you want mine. There *is* nothing else.'

She caught at him as he began to lift himself off her: 'Don't go, please don't stop.'

He paused. 'Is that a retraction?'

Julia couldn't believe that he could stop now, that he would deprive them both of satisfaction if she didn't lie to him. He didn't want her love—she could understand that—but to do this . . . 'No.'

She felt the tortured shudder of his body and for a moment she thought he was giving in. Then, sweat breaking out on an impassive face, he pulled away and sat up, reaching for his trousers on the floor.

'Oh God, I don't believe you. You won't make love to me because I said "I love you"? You're incredible! Is this some new morality I haven't heard of?'

'Not new. Mine. You know the score, Julia, or you should.' He was referring to her supposed experience. Now was definitely not the time to confess to none. She knelt up on the bed, the flush of their love-making still mantling her body. He, too, was still aroused, and moved stiffly as he dressed and walked over to poke viciously at the dying fire. Julia followed him, naked and pleading, her body gleaming as flames leapt anew in the grate.

'Are you afraid? Is that it? You think I'll make demands on you? Won't you . . .'

'No, Julia!' he turned his back to her. 'Don't compound the error. Put on your clothes and go.'

'Why, Hugh? Why?' she asked quietly, not moving. 'I didn't ask for anything in exchange.'

'No, but you expect it all the same; if not now, later,' he said perceptively. 'It was a mistake, Julia. I don't want to get involved, and neither should you.'

'It's too late, I am involved,' Julia moved around to confront him proudly, tossing her golden head. She would not allow him to make her ashamed of what she felt or what they had done. 'I love you, Hugh . . . all of you, even as you are now . . . and there's not a damned thing you can do about it.'

'Put your clothes on,' he said, ignoring her challenge, though the grey eyes had to wrench themselves away from the inviting loveliness before him.

She was tempted to say 'make me' but she sensed that confrontation was not going to work after all. Silently she pulled her clothes over suddenly chilled flesh. She gave the evocative hollow in the wide bed one last wistful glance.

'All right, I'll go,' she said quietly. 'But don't think it changes anything. I love you. I'm not asking you to change what you are; I'm not asking you for pretty lies. Maybe I will get hurt, but that's my risk, Hugh, not yours. You risk nothing.'

He closed his eyes as if he as in pain and for a moment Julia though she had reached him. But:

'No, no more, Julia.' It was said with such weary bleakness that Julia retired, defeated, without another word. Left the tall, broad-shouldered man shrouded by the shadows of his room, and by deeper, darker shadows, that she could know nothing about. Left him brooding, alone—as he meant always to be.

CHAPTER NINE

I MUST have no sense of occasion, thought Julia next morning as she lay abed contemplating another pure and frosty day, no sense of tragedy. She had slept like a log and her pillow was redolent with dreams rather than tears. By rights she should be feeling shattered, instead she felt oddly optimistic.

Oh, they had shared some beautiful moments up there in Hugh's eyrie. Golden moments ... glorious, unforgettable. Julia stretched languorously as she relived their deliciousness.

She simply would not accept his rejection. The fact that Hugh hadn't continued to make love to her after her too-ready confession of love was actually in her favour. If he had not given a damn for her he would have gone ahead regardless. Julia knew that most men, given a willing woman, wouldn't quibble about a few whispered love words. But Hugh cared too much for his own self-respect, and hers, to lie. And, too, he was afraid. Afraid of love and everything it entailed. Something had happened to destroy his faith in emotions. His rigid self-control, his obsession with privacy, his contempt for sentimentality, all these feelings were rooted in the past. They must be very deeply ingrained to have survived a long, loving apprenticeship with the Marlows. Julia had her own suspicions, but they could only be guesses.

She didn't regret what she had done. She could no more have held back her confession of love than she could have stopped breathing. In the midst of joy and passion she had been true to herself. And because she loved him she could forgive Hugh his brutality, knowing it was her, Julia, he was rejecting, so much as the idea of love itself.

141

She frowned, and bounced determinedly out of her bed. There were still—she counted on her fingers—still seven days of her employment left. Surely in that time she could slip under Hugh's defences, persuade him that she was mature enough to make the transition from friend to lover without threatening his emotional status quo. Let him then discover for himself the satisfaction of a close-bond with someone who loved him enough to enjoy giving more than taking.

But what if she was wrong about him? Julia worried as she dressed. What if he was truly incapable of giving anything of himself into a sustained relationship? She chewed her lip thoughtfully. If raw sex was all he could ever offer, could she settle for that, for being only a minor part of his life? But then, sex with Hugh hadn't been raw, even if he had intended it to be so. He had tempered its heat with consideration and unselfishness. He had loved her with his body . . . surely at some level he was capable of loving her with his mind? She longed to make him happy, to bring him smiles and laughter, to fill the clinical corners of his carefully structured life with warmth. She wanted to drive away for even the grim emptiness that she had glimpsed in his face last night, as he turned her away.

Julia made herself slow down as she prepared and then cleaned up after breakfast. The croissants were softly crisp from the oven, the kedgeree a creamy-hot concoction of savoury goodness, the waffles chewy and sweet. She ate a double-helping herself, to curb her impatience. Don't push, she told herself. Hugh hates to be pressured. Take it slow, marshal your arguments, slay him with logic if not love. There was no *logical* reason that she and Hugh shouldn't become lovers.

Monday was laundry day and Julia was washing up the last few dishes as Jean Brabbage sailed through the kitchen with another load of bed linen.

'I may as well clean Mr Hugh's room while I'm here,' she commented as she came back. 'I hate to disturb him while he's at work so I'll grab the chance while he's away.'

Julia almost dropped the glass bowl she was drying and stared, heart pounding, at the plump expanse of olive-green wool that stretched across the housekeeper's back as she rummaged in the cleaning cupboard.

'Away? Away where?' she managed faintly.

'Auckland, so Mrs Marlow says,' said Jean, turning around. 'Business.' She sniffed. 'I thought he was down here to avoid business.'

'So did I,' said Julia numbly. 'For how long, do you know?'

'Three or four days, I think.' She bustled out of the room happily, unaware of Julia's misery.

Gone! And without even saying goodbye. The joy drained out of the day. Julia couldn't imagine that Hugh had been driven away by what had happened last night, or rather, by what hadn't happened. So it must just be an awful coincidence—an urgent call from his office perhaps. Or his publisher. There were dozens of possibilities, none of them likely to be you, Julia told herself sternly. The day-to-day business of the world didn't stop just because Julia Fry had fallen in love!

But when would she see him again? And what would she say? What would *he* say? Would things be the same between them, or different? Please, please don't let us be back at square one, Julia agonised. Three or four days! The suspense was going to kill her. She could only hope that a few days away might result in Hugh's discovery that he missed her. She clung to the thought.

Whichever way her doubts carried her, she certainly didn't expect what actually happened. Hugh arrived on Tuesday evening, an hour or so before dinner. Gathered in the lounge for drinks, the family heard the throaty purr of the Maserati in the driveway and looked expectantly at the door as footsteps sounded in the hallway. Julia put down her glass with a hand that trembled.

It wasn't Hugh, though, who came through the lounge door first. It was the elegantly groomed figure of Ann Farrow. Julia's throat slammed closed and she struggled for breath.

'My dear!' Connie recovered herself first and rose regally from the couch, throwing an enquiring look at her son as he towered in the doorway. 'How nice to see you again so soon.'

'Ann's staying for a few days, Connie,' Hugh said meeting her eyes blandly. 'I knew you wouldn't mind my inviting her.'

'Why, no, of course not,' said Connie gamely, clinging determinedly to her self-possession. She looked helplessly at her husband, who raised an eyebrow, and back to Ann. 'You can have the room next to us—Ros can move in with Olivia, can't you, darling? Come and have a drink you two, it must be freezing outside. Sit down, Ann.'

'Thank you.' Ann's voice was a cultured drawl and she moved with the self-confidence of beauty. She's got hard eyes, though, thought Julia critically, as she watched Hugh guide his guest to the couch with a hand under her elbow. She felt outraged when he followed her down and the two of them sat, thighs touching, presenting a smugly combined front to the rest of the room.

'Fortunately I don't have any classes this week,' Ann continued, sending Julia's spirits into a further nose-dive. 'It's nice to get away from the intensity of the campus now and then. When Hugh asked me to come down with him for a few days, naturally I couldn't resist.'

Naturally. Julia stared at her with dislike. She had never been jealous of anyone or anything before in her life, yet now the emotion seethed hotly inside her. She sat and slowly steamed as everyone gradually recovered their manners and filled the room with conversation, unable to utter a word. The way she felt, if she opened her mouth she would shriek like a fishwife. It was obvious to the meanest intelligence what Hugh was doing. He was making a definite statement. He had said that Julia wasn't a subtle person, but what Hugh was doing wasn't just unsubtle, it was downright cruel.

He only met her gaze once, and Julia's eyes shot cobalt sparks that were politely ignored. He even smiled slightly; the bastard! If anything it was that superficial smile that convinced Julia that she was right. He was brandishing Ann like a shield. Ann was of his world; Ann was a sensible, sophisticated woman, she wouldn't embarrass a man with protestations of love. Hugh didn't like scenes, but Julia was going to give him one. He needn't think he could scare her off by flaunting another woman in her face. Julia didn't scare easily.

When he excused himself to take his luggage upstairs, Julia seized her chance, and muttered something about dinner. She caught him as he turned the first landing.

'Hugh!'

He half-turned, foot on the first of the next flight of stairs. 'Julia?'

She sought for an opening gambit. 'Do you want me to come up after dinner? You must be behind with your schedule again by now.' She hadn't meant it to sound quite so accusing.

'That won't be necessary. Ann is going to do some proof-reading for me.'

'Oh, so she came down here to *work*,' said Julia sarcastically. 'Why couldn't I proof-read?'

'Do you have a degree in English?'

'I though she was a computer specialist.'

'She also has an English degree.'

'I suppose she can type too,' Julia muttered sullenly.

'No. But I can.' He held up his hand and wiggled the healed fingers in proof. 'So I think that we can now dispense with your valuable services.' He took another step and Julia exploded against the door he was trying to shut in her face.

'Now wait a minute, buster.' She dashed up the stairs in front of him and whirled around to bar his way with her small figure. Their faces were on a level for once and it gave Julia a feeling of confidence. Hugh looked as calm as ever, but Julia sensed that he was braced against attack, the grey eyes wary. 'I demand to know what is going on here!'

The corners of his mouth turned down. 'I'm taking my case up to my room. Any objection?'

'Yes, I have an objection, several of them as a matter of fact,' said Julia, incensed by his literalism, enough to plunge to the heart of the problem. 'What did you bring *her* down for?'

'If by *her* you mean Ann,' he said, knowing she did, 'why shouldn't I? She's a close friend of mine . . . she's often helped me with my work. Must I now have permission from the household staff before I can invite my friends to visit me?'

'Hah!' Julia flung back her head in disbelief. 'Sarcasm doesn't become you, Hugh. Or are you ashamed to have sunk to the level of seducing servants?'

'Don't be ridiculous, Julia,' he said at his coldest, attempting to retrieve his mistake.

'Yes isn't it,' she said sweetly. 'Whatever you are you're not a snob. So why the sudden coyness? You seduce me and then slink off like a thief in the night, and then come back with Miss Computer in tow. Is this another example of Mr G.B.H. Walton's infamous morality?'

'Let's not debate who did what to whom . . .' he began.

'Who? *Whom?*' Julia cut him off, swooping sarcastically. 'There's no need to be so careful with your grammar, *I'm* not the English scholar; *I'm* just a poor, ignorant cook. I'm not one of your cerebral types who can be fobbed off with fine words. I'm Julia. I'm me, and I don't give up so easily.' Her fierceness gave her stature, her determination an almost visible aura around her stiffly-held golden head.

'There is nothing to give up,' Hugh pointed out with clipped precision. 'And you flatter yourself if you think that Ann's presence has anything to do with you. The world doesn't revolve around your rather unstable emotions, you know.'

Julia wavered. It sounded nonsensical said out loud. Instinct came to her aid. She was not a vain person but she knew, deep in her bones, that Hugh was strongly attracted to her. He was bluffing, and with his face he was a master of bluff.

'I thought you said you came down here to work on your own ... to get away from the pressures of your office? If you were so keen on having Miss Farrow's help, why didn't you ask her to stay last time she was here?'

'I didn't need her then. Frankly, Julia, I don't see why I should be answerable to you for my actions.'

'Don't you just?' Julia glared at him, baffled. 'All I want is a straight answer.' She tried a final dig: 'If you're afraid of me, confront it ... tell me I scare you to death.'

'More Freud?' he asked softly. 'All right, have it your way, Julia. I'm scared to death of you ...' and, without a pause '... I hope you can stretch dinner to two extra.' Leaving Julia open-mouthed behind him he took the rest of the stairs two at a time.

Julia snapped her mouth shut. Very clever, Hugh Walton. She couldn't quite grasp how he had eluded her. He had admitted his feat, but with such smooth insincerity that no one in their right mind would believe him. Unfortunately for him, Julia wasn't in her right mind. She was in love.

Over the next few days her love had to put up with great adversity. Ann fitted herself very neatly into the family circle. She would fit herself neatly into any situation, Julia thought sourly, for all her intelligence she had no real personality of her own, it had been honed almost out of existence.

It was galling, though, to see what a perfect couple she and Hugh made—both tall and handsome, treating each other with the comfortable intimacy of long acquaintanceship. Julia couldn't hope to compete with Ann on an intellectual level, that much was obvious from the long, obscure conversations that she and Hugh had indulged in over dinner, successfully excluding everyone else. Julia, back between the twins and now treated to a friendly camaraderie tinged, to her chagrin, with sympathy, felt like an ignorant clodhopper in comparison. It made her wonder whether Ann, with her sleek self-satisfaction, her slight air of hardness, might not be a better match for Hugh in the long run.

Yet, watching them, Julia could detect no sign of deep-running passion between them, no silent strands of communication. She knew for a fact herself that Hugh was no stranger to voluptuary—he had proved that more than once. Julia couldn't imagine Ann ever abandoning herself to feeling. She seemed to be the opposite of sensuous, filtering everything through her brain. Hugh was different. For real fulfilment he would require more from a woman than mere compliance, or intellectual stimulation. He needed a different kind of woman, one who could help cross-pollinate that rigidly departmentalised personality of his. *Someone like me,* Julia thought.

One afternoon, as Julia rooted around in the weedy vegetable patch, searching for the tender remains of the brussels sprouts, she was caught off guard by the unexpected appearance of her arch rival, who rarely ventured out of the house unless in the passenger seat of the Maserati.

'You enjoy gardening do you?' she enquired in tones which equated it on a level with finger-painting.

Julia arched her aching back and managed a thin smile, conscious of her grubby denims and old navy sweater with holes in the elbows. Ann wore one of her wool suits, knife pleats and all. At least her condescension didn't extend to Julia's skill in the kitchen. Thumbing her nose at fate she had surpassed herself in the last three days, producing ever more delectable and complicated dishes. Last night she had stunned everyone's taste buds with her Maigret de Canard—thin slices of very rare duck served with bearnaise and bordelaise sauce—supplemented by a big tureen of green vegetables layered with scallops and hollandaise sauce. While they were still in a state of shock she had followed it up with her killer: pineapple flamed with Tia Maria served with vanilla ice-cream sprinkled with fresh-cracked pepper. The repast had pierced even Ann's blasé façade. Hugh hadn't commented, but he had eaten every bite and Julia had been reassured by his evident appreciation of the whole sensual experience.

'You finish here in a couple of days, don't you? Going back with everyone else?' Ann asked, with a casualness belied by the fact she had actually sought Julia out.

'Yes.' Julia stabbed savagely at a sprout.

'I'll be staying on, of course, with Hugh. Just for a few days, to help with his book. Hugh and I are friends from way back.'

'So Connie said,' Julia forced out through numb lips. She should have seen this coming.

'Did she?' Julia could practically hear the wheels clicking. Does she think that Connie's accepted the inevitable, on the strength of a few days' visit? Does she think she's in there with a chance? So why slog out here to hold a conversation with one of the educationally sub-normal? Hugh wouldn't go as far as *marrying* her, would he? Perhaps he would, not because he couldn't bear not to, but because it would be a practical way to protect himself from any future threat to his equilibrium. A marriage of convenience.

'It was very good of you to help Hugh with his typing.' Now Ann was being kind. The knife twitched in Julia's hand. 'He told me how you shut his hand in the door.' She shuddered delicately. 'He must have been rather annoyed. It was typical of him to let you work out your apology.'

That puts me in my place. 'Yes, wasn't it. Actually he hit the roof when I did it. He yelled and cursed. I thought he was going to kill me.' She opened her blue eyes to their most fearful wideness. The slight rigidity of the older woman's expression told her she had struck a nerve. Ann had obviously never seen Hugh in one of his tempers. *Only I can rouse him to that,* thought Julia with satisfaction. 'Then he practically twisted my arm to get me to do his typing. He's so forceful and dominating; I love a man with a bit of fierceness in him.' The last half of that statement was entirely truthful.

'He has an extremely fine legal brain,' Ann said firmly, dismissing this unlikely aspect of Hugh. She watched painfully as Julia clumped off the garden with her bucket and paused to scrape off the mud which clung to her extremely large gumboots. Jean Brabbage's of course—her husband's would be several sizes smaller!

'You must realise that, to a man like Hugh, work is the central pivot to life.' *Did she lecture in this supercilious fashion?* Julia wondered. 'He needs the constant stimulation it provides for him, and he will always put it before everything else. That's why he needs tranquillity to come home to, not a constant barrage of distractions. Naturally, in his position he also has to maintain a certain standard of responsibility, particularly if he's planning a political career.'

She went on and on as she followed a smouldering Julia back to the house, stressing the importance of Hugh's career, and how clever he was. Strange how two women could see a single man so differently, Julia thought. Ann patently believed every word she said, and heartily approved of Hugh-the-automaton. But it

was *because* Julia didn't believe he was really like that
that she loved him. Are we both projecting our own
needs on to him? she worried. Does Hugh only exist as
we perceive him? Or has he a separate existence which
neither of us can see or understand? If she could see
him, talk to him alone, she might be able to resolve
some of her confusion.

Chance was a fine thing. Hugh had perfected the art
of avoiding people, and unwelcome confrontations. Julia
was frustrated at every turn, but a brief conversation
with Connie persuaded her to force the issue.

'He's not really serious about her, is he?' Connie
mourned to her, the day before the exodus fom
Craemar. 'I mean, honestly, at least I used to be able to
rely on Hugh's predictability. Lately he's been
impossible. I thought perhaps you ...' she trailed off
with unaccustomed delicacy, raising her eyebrows
expectantly.

Julia was warmed by her partisanship, but compelled
to say: 'I thought Ann was getting on rather well with
all of you.'

'And straining at the seams in the process,' Connie
said acidly. 'She comes from an old family, you know,
and silly as it seems in this day and age I think she feels
that the Marlows are a little *outré*. She has these
fantasies about Hugh ... and you must admit it isn't *de
rigueur* for a New Zealand Prime Minister to have an
actress for a mother and a rock singer for a brother.'

Julia gave her a strained grin. 'You sound as
pompous as Hugh sometimes.'

'I know, darling. Infectious isn't it? But can you
imagine Ann putting up with us on an in-law basis?
And we see little enough of Hugh as it is.'

'She sticks to him like glue!' Julia burst out. 'And he
hardly ever talks to me anymore.'

'She's scared, poor thing. Not half as confident as she
looks—though she's got the hide of an armadillo, and
an equal amount of sensitivity. Like me to draw her off

for you, so you can sink a word in edgeways?' She tossed out the invitation casually.

'Would you? I mean . . . there's something that *needs* to be said.' She would explode like an over-heated pressure cooker soon, if she didn't.

'Of course there is,' said Connie placidly. 'This afternoon, after lunch.' And at the nervous gleam in Julia's eye: 'I'll be the soul of discretion, darling.'

For once she was. As they rose from lunch Connie corralled her victim and bore her off to Michael's study to read his play: 'Being an English Honours, I'm sure you're interested. It's about the conflict between machines and man . . . there's a marvellous part in it for me . . .'

They had barely passed through the study door before Julia was upstairs, knocking tentatively at Hugh's door.

'Come in, Ann,' came the call, and Julia was pleased to hear the barely disguised impatience. So Ann wasn't welcome any time of the day or night!

Her appearance earned her a double-take. 'Julia!' He recovered at once. 'What do you want? I'm very busy.'

'I'll wait.' She walked over to the fire, deliberately picking his wing chair to sit in, scuffing off her shoes and tucking her feet up.

With a sigh he carefully capped his pen and laid it down, centring it precisely on the papers in front of him. But he made no move to get up. 'What is it that's so important?'

'You. Me. Us. And her. She's a bore.'

'Ann is extremely intelligent.'

'And beautiful,' agreed Julia. 'An extremely intelligent, beautiful *bore*. The conversation must be riveting when you're alone. Do you sit and stroke each other's egos?'

'Isn't this a bit childish, Julia?' he asked tightly. Julia wondered if she had struck a nerve.

'On the contrary.' She gave him a provocative look.

'We've been over this . . .'

'No we haven't. You wouldn't let us. You'd rather bury your head in the sand . . . or should I say hide behind one hundred per cent woollen skirts, imported, *naturally*,' she parodied the drawl. 'Why can't you be honest with me?'

He leaned back in his chair, eyes narrowed on her small face, purified by the white light of the spot above her head. 'But I have been honest. You just won't accept it. I admit that on an elemental level I find you attractive, but not overwhelmingly so, as Sunday night should have told you. Consider it a momentary aberration.'

'Aberration, nothing!' cried Julia, furious at his coolness. 'And it wasn't momentary either. We were both naked and in *your* bed. The only reason we aren't lovers is because you're afraid of the depth of your own desires. Or else you're a virgin, which I doubt, from your expertise!'

'Don't make this harder than it is, Julia.'

'I want to go to bed with you, you want to go to bed with me. I don't see what's so hard about that,' she persisted, pushing small, clenched fists against her thighs. She mustn't let him steamroll her.

'Then you're even more naive than I thought. What you want, I can't give.'

'What does it matter what I want? It's what *you* want that matters,' she cried, her voice thin and high.

'Is it?' He shifted sceptically in his chair, and it creaked mournfully. 'How self-sacrificing of you. But I make it a rule not to have sex with women who believe themselves in love with me.'

Have sex? Believe? How often did it happen, for God's sake? Julia battled her rage. He was still avoiding the issue.

'All right,' she said gently. 'Let's pretend I'm not in love with you.'

He removed his hands from the desk, hiding them

behind the barrier of the desk. Julia remembered what it was like to have them drifting across her body, cupping her breasts, stroking a lazy path to her thighs. *Oh, Hugh.*

'That's not possible.'

'Why?'

'Haven't you found solace already?'

'What?' Julia was bewildered by the harshness of the sudden accusation.

'I saw you, the other night, coming out of Richard's room.'

'Spying?' she demanded, her heart leaping. Was he jealous?

'Passing by.'

'You're not going to bring up that hoary old groupie theory again, are you?' she scoffed. 'Richard and I aren't lovers, never have been. He was *trying* to take my mind off your rotten behaviour. He knows I'm in love with you.'

'No, Julia. You're in love with some kind of image of me that you've created in your own head.'

'God, I wish I was,' said Julia fervently, having considered, and finally dismissed the idea herself. 'A fantasy Hugh would be so much more accommodating than you are. I even love the beast in you.'

He flinched. 'And what about your pathetic attempts to thrust me into the bosom of my family? Isn't that trying to make me someone I'm not. Trying to make me into the kind of man you *expect* to love?'

'I'm not trying to change you. Just to discover who you really are. To help free you from whatever it is in your past that stops you from loving, or letting yourself be loved . . .'

'What in the hell do you know of the past!' His savage ferocity forced Julia back into her chair, even as he rose violently to his feet, his own chair crashing over with the movement. 'I'll say it again, Julia, I am what I am. Don't meddle with what you don't understand.

Stay out of my life! Keep your damned inquisitiveness to yourself!'

'It's not inquisitiveness!' Julia wasn't afraid. She preferred this to his punishingly logical calmness. 'It's because I care. I know you didn't have a very happy childhood——'

He gave a hoarse laugh. 'I don't need your pity, Julia, any more than I need your love,' he ground out. 'Don't feel sorry for me. I'm precisely where I want to be.' There was loathing in his very contemplation of her pitying him.

Julia got up and moved towards him, speaking passionately: 'I don't. Oh, I feel sorry for the boy, that scrawny twelve-year-old who took up weightlifting to escape the bullies. But not for the man. I don't pity the man. You've made yourself into something that doesn't need pity. I may not like the things you are, but that doesn't change the way *I* am. That doesn't stop me wanting or loving you. And don't fool yourself that you can do without love entirely, Hugh. Without love you wouldn't be here today. You wouldn't have Connie or Michael, or your brothers and sisters. If you deny love, you deny them; and you don't really want to do that, Hugh, do you? You want the best of both worlds. You want love but you don't want to have to acknowledge or understand it. Hugh . . . *Hugh!*'

The last was a desperate plea. She came right up to him and struck him on the iron chest with her tiny fist. As she touched him a shudder passed through his body and she shuddered also, as if his anger, his pain, his tortured confusion passed physically over to her. She felt it as if it was her own. Hugh was staring at her, not seeing, and his hands came slowly up to rest on the close, curving arch of her hipbones and grip hard, clenching, as if he would wring the love from her body.

Instinctively Julia arched towards him, pulling his head down with her fists on his shoulders, going up on her toes to kiss him, groaning with satisfaction as his arms went around her and he held her so tightly her bones ached. For long, long moments they were locked in a desperate embrace as he yielded to hot, urgent passion. The large hands slid to the small of her back, pulling her soft thighs against him. He was as hard as iron, driven by her sweetness into unleashing his demons upon her. He used her roughly, but not hurtfully, and she was exultant at his surrender.

But then, at her moment of triumph, he suddenly tore himself out of her arms, white-faced, and stared at her in a kind of tormented horror.

'No. No.' He scrubbed his mouth with the back of a shaking hand, wiping out the ecstasy of the last few minutes, speaking raggedly, the soft voice splintered with purpose. 'I refuse to do something that we can only regret.'

He was gone. Slamming out of the room, out of her life ... and this time it was Julia who was left alone to contemplate an empty future.

CHAPTER TEN

'I THINK you've been putting on a little weight,' Phillip Randolph ran a critical eye over Julia as he came into the kitchen after farewelling the last of his dinner guests. He had been back for three weeks, entertaining almost every night, and Julia had avidly welcomed the intense activity. She was uneasily aware that for the first time in her career she was looking on cooking as a distraction, rather than as the main focus of her life.

And it wasn't working.

'I have to *taste* the food, Phillip,' she snapped sarcastically, slamming down a pan.

Phillip backpedalled hastily: 'I didn't mean that as a criticism ... you look ... er ... extremely well.'

'Good, because I think you've put on some weight yourself. Must have been all that high-calorie Continental food.'

Phillip glanced down at himself, alarmed. 'Do you think so?' He tugged nervously at his waistcoat and Julia sighed. What a bitch she was.

'Only kidding, Phillip, you're as sleek as ever. Well-fed, but sleek.'

He relaxed, reassured, and Julia sighed again. She shouldn't take out her frustrations on Phillip. She *had* put on weight. Other people pined away for love, but Julia's metabolism reacted with characteristic waywardness. She was hungry, constantly, a burning, nervous, compulsive hunger and she ate to reassure herself that she really was alive. She didn't feel alive, she felt desiccated, shrivelled, she felt *thin*. It was a shock to look in the mirror every morning expecting to see a gaunt skeleton and be confronted instead with a blooming image. Her body was firm and resilient, her eyes sparkled, her hair shone. It was the exercise that did it ... she had been forced to take up jogging, which she loathed intensely, to keep herself down to a reasonable size. Every time she went out, torturing her body with speed and distance, she was torturing her mind with memories, and, over and over, the futile question *why?*

Right up until the end she had been confident that she could reach him, that there was a way but that she was too inexperienced, too ignorant to find it; that given time she would. But time had run out on her, and with it her shining dreams.

Why? Why? the question was pounded out on the neighbourhood pavements. Because he was afraid? Afraid of what? Some future hurt? Surely his logic should tell him that all of life is a gamble. He wasn't a coward. Cautious, perhaps, but not a coward. Didn't his instinct tell him that she would never, never hurt him? Obviously not.

Ironically, her last sight of him had been almost an exact reverse of the first ... in her rear vision mirror, slowly dwindling to disappear as she turned the bush-lined curve of Craemar's driveway. Until that moment she had truly believed that he would relent. How wrong she had been; completely, shatteringly, excruciatingly wrong, throwing into doubt everything she thought she had known about him.

She had wanted to turn around and drive straight back, to confront him, but it wasn't just pride that restrained her. Ann Farrow had been standing beside Hugh under the portico as he farewelled his family, probably well aware of the elegantly framed picture they made. The perfect couple. Julia's own goodbye, perforce a formal, public one had rung sickeningly hollow in her ears.

She had cried, on and off, all the way back to Auckland, stopping at laybys every now and then to wipe away the blinding tears with a sodden handkerchief. She wanted to hate him; oh, how she longed for a nice, cleansing hatred, but it wasn't in her nature to be bitter and her compassionate heart felt such pain for Hugh that it almost equalled that she felt for herself. She had so much love to give, and such a longing to give it. If Hugh had opened his heart and mind to her she could have enriched both their lives.

Why?

She had looked forward in desperation to Phillip's return, but the rash of dinner parties he initiated hadn't been the magic formula for recovery. Her concentration was affected, though she was too much a professional to let it show in her superb meals. Her hands performed their duties mechanically while her mind roamed wild and free.

All about her spring was breaking into bud, the new growth emphasising the wintry bleakness that remained within, the stunted limbs of what had promised to be such a glorious blossoming. Julia forced herself into a new awareness of her environment, the small, precious gifts of nature: the fragile, fragrant freesias that burst upon the air; the tiny, tentative, lime-green leaves unfurling on the stark oak trees at the bottom of the garden; the soft, warm caress of the spring breezes. The sadness that clung to her threw each individual moment of pleasure into sharp relief, intensifying her need to discover a reason for hope. Spring was that reason, the endless cycle of renewal. There was a season for everything, Julia knew, and this was her season for weeping.

Gradually, as she sought a path through pain, and anger, and confusion, she became convinced of one thing. That her love for Hugh, though it would fade and change with the years, would always be a part of what she was, of the life she made for herself. And she wanted it to be so. She couldn't discard a love because it wasn't returned; the beauty of the freesia was no less beautiful for being fleeting, the miracle of the leaf no less a miracle because it would wither in order to save the tree.

'So, what do you think, Julia?'

'What?' She stared blankly at Phillip. Had he been talking all this time?

'You haven't heard a word I've said!' he accused, unused to such inattention. 'I said I'm thinking of taking up permanent residence in the Caribbean.'

'The Caribbean!' echoed Julia stupidly. Was Philip taking up beachcombing?

'For tax purposes.' He explained it all again, with a sarcastic slowness that was an accusation in itself. 'I wouldn't have to live there the whole year round, just long enough to establish resident status.'

'Is this a roundabout way of telling me I'm fired?'

'Pay attention, Julia! I want you to come with me, that's what this whole conversation is about!'

Julia ignored his irritation. A couple of months ago she would have been over the moon, but now the first thought that popped into her head was how far the Caribbean was from Hugh Walton. By straining credulity she could imagine Hugh seeking her out in Auckland, but going with Phillip would really be burning her boats—patched and leaky as they were!

'You don't seem very enthusiastic.'

'Yes, well ...' she said, trying to summon some animation, '... could I think it over?'

'Of course,' he said stiffly. 'There's a considerable amount of red tape to go through yet, and the real estate firm haven't found me a suitable location yet. I certainly won't be moving until the new financial year.'

'I'm sorry, Phillip,' said Julia, conscious of having offended him once again. 'The idea of the Caribbean is fantastic, but all my family's here, and I've had my years of travelling.' Now all she wanted to do was settle down with the right man!

'Good Lord, Julia, you sound middle-aged! What's come over you the last few weeks?'

'It's spring, maybe I'm feeling the nesting instinct.' She ventured the truth under guise of lightness.

'Richard Marlow, I suppose,' Phillip pounced scornfully. 'I wouldn't bank on him too much if I was you. Actors are inclined to be a bit unstable. You can't rush into these things without considering the practicalities, Julia.'

Julia gritted her teeth at his condescending tone. Why shouldn't she rush in? Love should be spontaneous, not planned out like a financial campaign. Anyway, Phillip was wrong, she had had plenty of time to work out all the practical details of living with Hugh.

First, she would move into his apartment; then find a job with more reasonable hours—maybe catering for private lunches. She would insist on financial independence, respect the more entrenched of Hugh's solitary habits, do his typing if he asked nicely. If there were children (perhaps a girl who could become a lawyer, and a boy to be a chef!) she would become an enthusiastic, housewifely mother, at least while they were young. God, what bliss it would be to have such beautiful certainties in her future!

Observing her drift into a daydream Phillip let the subject drop, but he didn't let her forget. He took to leaving brightly coloured travel brochures lying casually around the house. Julia didn't even bother to read them. She knew the problem wouldn't go away just because she ignored it, but she couldn't bring herself to seriously think about it.

She had promised Connie when they left Craemar that she would keep in touch, but somehow it didn't happen. Julia felt that, though she hadn't said anything, in some indefinable way she had let Connie down. The feeling seemed to be confirmed as the weeks passed and she didn't hear from *any* of the Marlows. She read in the papers that rehearsals for *Romeo and Juliet* had begun, so she excused Richard on the grounds of work, though it had never stopped him before.

She also learned from the newspapers that *Hard Times* had cancelled its concert tour of the Far East, and that Steve was immersed in the composition of a rock opera, to be performed by the group in conjunction with one of Auckland's professional theatres.

From the *Arts* section of one of Phillip's glossy magazines she discovered that Olivia Marlow ('promising young Auckland artist') had received a grant to study for a year in Paris under the aegis of a famous French tutor. The grant, made through the Queen Elizabeth II Arts Council, was by an anonymous donor. Hugh? Julia's throat thickened with tender yearning as the page blurred before her eyes. The timing was right, and who else would be so anxious to hide an impulse of generosity? Dear, darling Hugh. Where was he now? And with whom? She sniffed fiercely at the thought of the wretched Farrow woman. A man who preferred a woman like that deserved everything he got. It probably wouldn't have worked anyway—a relationship with Hugh—Julia lectured herself sternly. A one-sided love was doomed from the start. And they were such fundamentally different people. They probably would have spent all their spare time arguing. All the time they spent out of bed, that is.

Julia caught herself up on the slip. 'Out, out, damned spot,' she muttered as she answered the doorbell late one evening. She must concentrate on the negative things about Hugh, the things she didn't like: the secretiveness, the intermittent coldness, the ease with which he ignored people ... the ... the ... oh, what was the use! when all she really wanted to remember was the sweet warmth of his breath on her body, the silken sweep of those large, gentle hands, the heady excitement of feeling him pressing against her, the times when he made her laugh, when he made her think.

It wa a shock to throw open the door and find Richard standing sheepishly outside. As if her thoughts had conjured up a Marlow, even if it was the wrong one.

Richard greeted her cheerily and was inside, chatting about the play, and the family, making himself at home before she had a chance to open her mouth. Finally he paused.

'And how are you? You look . . . blooming.'

'So I should be,' said Julia, thinking of all that damned exercise. She was sitting on the couch, hands clasped loosely on her stomach and she gasped as she followed his suspicious gaze. 'No, I'm not! Fancy even thinking it!'

'These things happen in the best of families.'

'Not unless you're God.'

'What!' Richard's nimble mind alerted. 'Julia! You're not still a *virgin* are you?'

'You look more shocked than you did when you thought I was pregnant,' Julia complained, embarrassed at his astonishment.

'But . . . I . . . we all naturally assumed . . .'

'It never got that far. Not for want of trying on my part,' admitted Julia with a painful honesty. How she had tried!

' "She burnes that never knew desire,
    She that was ice, she now is fire." '

Richard lapsed into quotation, but his voice held sympathy as well as knowledge and Julia was hard put not to burst into tears. How well that described the state she was in, the heated turmoil of her thoughts and feelings.

'Well, here's something that might cheer you up, the reason I came,' said Richard, fumbling in his jacket pocket. Julia was too het-up to notice his unusual lack of curiosity. She didn't want to talk about it anyway or she *would* be in tears. She hated the thought of being one of those clingy, weepy females.

'Here. Two tickets to our opening Friday night.

Connie gave them to me. Said she'd love to see you.
You'll be sitting next to the girls. There's a party
afterwards, too.'

Julia stared at the proffered tickets as if they might
bite.

'Hugh won't be there,' he said, with what she thought
was unnecessary callousness. 'He's going back down to
Craemar again for the weekend, editing something or
other.'

Back down? So he had been here, in Auckland, and
not contacted her. Another door slammed in her face.
Still, she avidly lapped up the crumb of information.

'Hey, what's this?' Richard found one of Phillip's
brochures. 'Thinking of running off into the wild blue?'

Julia told him about Phillip's plans.

'Will you go?' with sudden sharpness.

'Maybe,' she shrugged, annoyed with herself that
indecisiveness, which had never been part of her
makeup before, was becoming a trait. She frequently
dithered of late, even over a simple thing like the route
for her next jog.

She was sorry when Richard finally left. Loneliness
was also new to her. Up until now her life had been
very comfortable, she realised. No traumas, no
tragedies or great upheavals to test the mettle of her
character. Fate had obviously been saving up for the
Big One. She felt alone and afraid, struggling along,
trying to reconnect the flow of her life. She should look
on Hugh as a drug she had to get out of her system. But
like Steve she had to *want* and *need* to do it herself. At
least she didn't have his unbearable temptation of
having her particular drug easily available. For her it
was cold turkey all the way. The real, the deepest fear,
was the unanswerable one. She avoided even thinking
about it. What if she was one of those people fated only
to love once in their life, once and forever? Would she
ever find happiness with another man if all love was to
be measured by this one?

She went alone to the theatre, meeting Ros and Olivia and Steve in the foyer. It was lovely to join their friendly banter again and as they took their seats in the stalls, Julia congratulated Steve and Olivia on their respective coups. Steve was relaxed, happy and cautiously optimistic about his rock opera. Olivia was over the moon. Julia caught Ros's eye and tried not to grin as Olivia told her, in an incredulous voice, that Logan had had the nerve to suggest going with her ... splitting the grant and going halves on expenses.

Poor Logan, thought Julia as the lights dimmed. We worried about the wrong person. Olivia had a fair chunk of the Marlow ambition in her makeup. Everything rated a poor second to Art right now ... including spiritual gurus!

The play was an immense success, earning the players a standing ovation and when Richard joined them at the after-show supper in the bar, Julia rewarded him with an exuberant hug.

'Thank you, darling,' he grinned, his facy shiny with cold cream and congratulations. 'You didn't notice the set shiver as I went over the balcony did you? I thought the whole lot was going to come down on top of me. God, I'm hot and thirsty.' He snatched a glass from a passing tray and toasted: 'Those who are about to die ...'

Ros overrode the others' protests. 'Yes, there were a few rough edges; I noticed you fluff a line or three.'

'Trust you to notice,' Richard groaned. 'And Juliet nearly got the giggles when the balcony wobbled. Have you seen Michael? He's grinning like a Cheshire cat!' According to Richard his father always smiled most just before he lowered the boom.

'Probably because he's so pleased,' said Julia, causing the trio of Marlows to exchange tolerant looks. 'Well, I thought it was perfect. Cheers!' She raised her third, or was it her fourth, glass of sparkling wine? She was feeling much better, chasing melancholy away with make-believe.

At midnight the management announced regretfully that their licence did not permit the serving of any more alcohol, and the glittering throng began their exodus. Soon there remained only hard-core supporters and cast.

Julia, frayed by an excess of hilarity, took to sipping wine from a coffee cup in deference to the licensing laws. She was floating in a haze when she was pounced upon by Connie and borne away to the stuffy peace of a dressing room the size of a small wardrobe.

'Mine, would you believe,' Connie announced, subsiding on to a wooden chair. 'And I share this shoebox with two others! Such are the rewards of fame. Sometimes I can understand people wanting to become secretaries or . . . or . . . mechanics!'

Julia latched on to the familiar. 'Charley?'

'So you know about Charley? I mean Charles. Why am I always the last? Michael says he should be given his head, providing he gets good marks in School Certificate this year. And who am I to oppose Michael? But enough of my trials. Pull up that stool, darling, and let's have a chat. I hear you're off overseas again.'

Julia was glad to sit down. Her head had lost its centre of gravity and the world was beginning to revolve around her in a most peculiar fashion.

'Not necessarily. I haven't made up my mind yet.'

'Good. You don't want to rush into anything. Where precisely is Phillip going?'

'Probably the Virgin Islands,' said Julia, with grim humour.

'Mmmm . . .' Connie eyed her thoughtfully, drumming her fingers on a silk-clad knee. 'You've put on weight, Julia—it suits you. In fact you're looking marvellous. Too good to be true. I thought you were supposed to be madly and unhappily love with my son?'

'Richard?' The world stood still, but now it was her head that spun.

Connie gave an exaggerated sigh. 'No, dear girl. Hugh.'

'Oh. *Hugh*.' She frowned into her drink.

'Yes. *Hugh*. Do *concentrate*, Julia. It's important.'

'Not to him.' A wave of alcoholic depression swept over Julia. 'He says I'm in love with a figment of my own imagination. *Is* it so impossible to believe that I might love him, himself?' she demanded belligerently.

'Of course not, darling. *I* believe you,' Connie soothed. 'It's just that Hugh won't *allow* himself to admit it. Just as he wouldn't allow himself to make love to you!' Connie spread her hands in charming deprecation as Julia blushed scarlet.

'Forgive us our trespasses, Julia, but Richard and I happen to care very much about you, and Hugh. I realise that mothers are not supposed to poke their noses into their sons' sex lives, but this is a special case. He blossomed so beautifully there for a while, with you, now he's all closed up again. And he never talks about himself ... he's such a secretive person ...' Connie sighed, and for a moment she looked all her years and more, the life dying out of her eyes, her curving mouth pinched with an old pain.

'*Deepest wounds can least their feelings tell*. That's Hugh. His wounds run very, very deep, Julia, and it's quite reasonable that he should fight against being hurt again. Poor Hugh ...'

Julia was desperately trying to clear her muzzy brain and focus her attention on Connie's moving mouth. What was she saying? Poor Hugh? What about poor Julia? She struggled to discipline her thoughts. Connie said this was *important*.

'You've probably made an educated guess about Hugh's early background. I think you should know the *real* story. It's not really mine to tell, but Hugh never talks about it ... and it might help you make a few necessary decisions.'

She straightened, and narrowed her green eyes, looking off into the distance. 'Hugh never really had a chance. He was doomed to being hurt from the moment he was born.

'His father was an alcoholic; mean-spirited, weak in every way except the purely physical. He was a big man, and when he was drunk he was a wrecker, a destroyer. His wife, Lydia, was a quiet, shy, kindly woman ... I suppose you might call her one of life's natural victims. A dangerous combination.'

Connie told the story simply, plainly, but the very starkness emphasised the horror. The truth was infinitely crueller than the inventions of Julia's fertile imagination. A battered child, that much she had guessed. But for the rest ...

Over the years George Walton had turned his home into a living hell for his wife and child, enforcing his drunken tyranny with brutal strength. When sober he would be bitterly remorseful, begging for forgiveness, crying, pleading, promising to change. He never did, but Lydia Walton stayed with him, too passive, too cowed, or too ashamed to seek help in breaking out of the vicious circle. The family moved around a lot as George took on odd labouring jobs, never in one place long enough to arouse the suspicions of neighbours or school teachers.

'Can you imagine what it must have been like for Hugh?' Connie asked quietly. 'Growing up in an atmosphere like that? Watching his mother beaten time and time again, helpless to intervene ... being beaten into submission himself both physically and mentally. His father became a genius at punishments: locking him into cupboards for hours at a time, denying him meals for imagined offences, or forcing the boy to watch as he systematically destroyed everything that the child valued—books, toys, schoolwork, clothes. It got so Hugh didn't dare show an affection for anything, in case it was used as punishment against him. And then there were the beatings themselves—belt, bottle, hot iron ... whatever was to hand.'

Julia was shaken with a sickening, sobering hatred. Not only for the animal that could so torture an innocent child, but also for the gentle woman who had seen it all happen and done nothing. Why hadn't she had the guts to protect her son? Even if she herself couldn't leave her husband, she could have sent her son away. Instead she had turned him into a victim too.

'One night George went too far. Lydia went into hospital with a fractured skull, broken arms and ribs. Her lung was pierced and she developed pneumonia with all sorts of complications. Not surprising, considering that both she and the boy were suffering from malnutrition along with everything else. She had no reserves to draw on, Julia. She just gave up and died. But she did tell the whole sordid story to the police. I don't think she cared for herself . . . she was afraid for her son, she knew she wouldn't be there to shield him from the brunt of his father's frustration and anger as she had always tried to do before. I'm sure that she loved Hugh, and that she felt guilty for clinging on to him. I think she had shut out all the pain and ugliness by trying to live through her son, her only joy in a joyless world.'

Oh, Hugh, my darling, was Julia's anguished, internal cry as Connie told her how he had finally ended up in the Marlow household, through the desperate offices of a friend in Social Welfare. It was a gamble, taken after Hugh had disrupted foster home after foster home, but it paid off. Connie had done a lot of work with disadvantaged children, for charity, as a means of occupying her time after the twins were born, and she and Hugh had seemed to 'click'. Perhaps it was the twins themselves, smaller and more helpless even than he, that helped Hugh come to terms with a wide, bewildering world, or perhaps it was the death of his father . . . the final threat removed.

'Either way, he never looked back,' Connie remembered. 'He developed by leaps and bounds, discovered his brain, built a sense of self-esteem, lost his fear of authority. But there's always been something missing.' She leaned forward earnestly, urgently. 'He needs to learn to love and trust, as a *man*—emotionally, spiritually, intellectually and sexually. If he doesn't he'll settle on Ann or some ghastly clone and never reach his full maturity or discover his destiny as a well-rounded human being. That—or he'll stultify in bachelorhood. I don't want that for Hugh, he deserves so much more. He's a fine man and I want him to find peace, real inner peace, the kind that comes with loving and being loved.'

'Oh, Connie . . .' Julia looked at her helplessly, aware of the tears on her cheeks, but unembarrassed by them because Connie was crying silently too. 'I can't force him to trust me, to accept something he doesn't want . . .'

'But he *does* want it,' Connie cried. 'That's exactly why he's turned you away. Don't you see, don't you *see* what I've been trying to tell you. Follow the twisted reasoning: everything that he ever loved was taken from him, so he *dare* not love again, because what he loves, past experience tells him he will lose. On top of that there's this fear that what he doesn't lose he himself will destroy. He's not a fool, he's well-read and knowledge-able . . . and it's a well-publicised fact that often battered children grow up maladjusted, to become abusive parents *themselves* . . .'

Julia trembled on the verge of realisation. 'You mean . . .'

'I *mean* that he's afraid history will repeat itself. He forgets that he carries his mother's genes as well as his father's. He's put such effort into controlling his personality that he doesn't realise that the control is merely reinforcing a basically gentle nature. He desperately needs that last piece of self-knowledge. As long as he thinks he's capable of hurting those he loves, he'll deny love. Deny himself.'

Julia shook her head, which was suddenly aching badly. 'I don't see . . . all this doesn't mean that he loves *me.*'

'No? How do you know? But you could find out. For once and for all.' Connie clasped her hands, in a gesture of supplication. 'He'll be back here on Sunday night. Go and see him, Julia, *please*. If not for your own sake, then for his. Try and get him to see how wrong he is. We both know that he's as gentle as a lamb. Please, Julia. And don't be put off by his stone-face, just remember, as I do, that the more he feels the less he shows.'

'I don't know,' Julia whispered, overwhelmed with misgivings. It was all right for Connie, *she* wasn't the one risking yet another rejection. Julia didn't know how many her ego could take!

'I know it won't be easy, darling. And that you have your pride and feelings too. But if you *really* love him, you'll give it a try. Just think, if I'm right, and you succeed, you'll have a pearl beyond price. You'll have Hugh. And isn't he worth more than pride?'

CHAPTER ELEVEN

HAVE HUGH. The two seductive words had lost quite a lot of their magic. Julia shivered. Not all Charley's tinkering had succeeded in stopping up the VW's draughts. A damp chill sank into her bones and stayed there, niggling at her concentration.

She leaned forward in the driver's seat, as if she could urge the car faster with the momentum of her body, cursing herself for her impulsiveness. It was Connie's last warning that had done it:

> 'Our doubts are traitors,
> And make us lose the good we oft might win
> By fearing to attempt.'

Shakespeare had hit the nail on the head. Julia's doubts were a legion and she had been afraid to give them time to join ranks. She had waited only for grim, grey dawn and a measure of sobriety before flinging a bag into the car and setting off, leaving a garbled note of explanation for Phillip. He would be furious, but at the moment that was the least of Julia's worries.

She peered out through her misty windscreen as the little car was buffeted across the Hauraki Plains. Who said that spring had sprung? This was winter weather back with a vengeance. It had been raining steadily since she had left Auckland and it seemed as if she had been on the road for days, stiff and tense from the battle with the elements.

She should have waited for Hugh to come back to Auckland, of course, but patience wasn't one of Julia's strong points. Two days was two days too long. She had to know. Now. *Today.* So that she could start to plan the rest of her life ... Virgin Islands and all!

172

Connie's story haunted her. It explained so much. How smug I must have seemed to him at times, Julia thought sadly. How shallow. Mouthing platitudes about life and its meaning, so confident of the all-healing properties of love. What reason did Hugh have to trust in love? His mother's love had been no protection for either of them. She had died for the sake of love, or misguided loyalty, or whatever strange, twisted emotion had bound her to her husband.

No, it wasn't with soft words or sweet love that she would reach Hugh. In fact, she wasn't quite sure how she would do it. By blind instinct probably . . . that was the way she worked best. The thought of Charley—and Olivia—heartened her somewhat. The shell had cracked a little, perhaps it just needed a sharp tap in the right place to fall apart completely.

She wasn't surprised to see the AA sign in Kopu telling her that the road via Tapu was closed. She had planned on going the 'safe' way in any case, across the base of the peninsula and up the coast. It was further, but less hair-raising than the Tapu way.

Nonetheless, by the time she crossed the Tairua River Julia was a mass of nerves. The river below her was swollen; a rolling, threatening, muddy brown and all around her she noticed hillside slips. In some cases she had to steer around scatterings of clay and boulders on the narrow road. What if some came down on top of the car? She crawled along, not daring to hurry in the treacherous conditions, trying to batten down her fear.

She felt almost ill with relief when she turned off the coast road to head down into the valley. Mist lay heavy on the trees and Julia's teeth began to chatter as she neared her destination. What on earth had she allowed herself to be talked into? Hugh would eat her alive for interfering once again in his well-ordered life. He had already thrown her out of it twice! Julia moaned aloud. If she wasn't *more* afraid of turning back and risking the boulders she would give up the battle here and now, without a shot being fired.

It was raining harder still as she steered gingerly down the driveway at Craemar, a distant roll of thunder accompanying her arrival; rather appropriately, she thought. Her aching legs betrayed her as she sloshed over the swampy gravel and a spasm of cramp jerked her foot on the accelerator. The car shot forward and the wheel slipped in her sweaty hands. Desperately she grabbed at it but the VW skewed madly sideways, out of control, and slipped with a dull clunk into the shallow ditch that ran along the lower side of the drive where it sloped towards the stream.

Julia could have screamed. The back wheels spun uselessly in the mud. She gave up, turning off the ingition, and stared up towards the blind windows of the house. There was smoke coming from Hugh's chimney. His curtains were open but there was no sign of movement in the attic room. Julia looked at her watch—nearly one o'clock! It had taken her over five hours to make what was usually a three-and-a-half-hour journey. No wonder she felt like a wet rag! The mist and thunderously dark skies had forced her to use her headlights over the last few kilometres, and that had been an added strain.

Suddenly Julia saw a blurry figure in the rain coming from the garage. She wrenched open her door and squelched on to the grass, gasping as the large, cold drops of rain sliced through her thick sweater and jeans. She howled against the wind: 'Hugh?'

The figure veered towards her, wielding a large, black umbrella against the windy onslaught. As he came closer Julia saw Hugh's face, white and rainwashed against the collar of his dark oilskin coat; strained in disbelief.

'Julia? What . . .' There was a loud boom, and the ground shook beneath their feet. Julia screamed, and scuttled towards the only solid thing in a shifting world.

'My God, was that thunder?' she yelled. 'The storm must be directly above us.'

Hugh cocked his head. 'I don't think . . .' he broke off as a crashing, thrashing, roaring sound came to them through the sodden air, like a wild animal on the loose. He muttered sharply and started to run towards the house, dropping the umbrella and dragging Julia with him.

'What is it? A landslide?' she gasped, her words whipped away by the wind.

No answer. She was half-yanked, half-carried through the front door and hustled up the dim staircase.

'What's the noise? What's happening?' earned her another brisk shove in the back. 'Now look here . . .' She was propelled into the welcome warmth of Hugh's room and ignored as he shrugged out of his oilskin and strode over to the window that looked down over the front of the house.

Panting Julia followed him, going on tip-toes to peer through the rain-distorted glass, gaping with horror at the sight that met her eyes.

A sweeping wall of slurry was smashing through the lower end of the grounds where the stream had been, snapping trees like matchsticks, bulldozing a tangled mass of fern and undergrowth before it. Behind the wall came a churning, boiling, devouring flood of water which rushed with menacing speed up the slope towards them.

Julia made a choked sound. 'Will it reach the house?'

'I doubt it. We're on pretty high ground here.' Hugh's voice sounded rusty with disuse and Julia stared at the beloved profile, turning again with a cry as he added: 'Unfortunately your car isn't.'

'Oh no!' The brown waters swirled around the VW, nudging it slightly adrift, seething greedily around the bonnet. The roaring sound eased to mingle with the drum of the rain and Julia, who had had visions of climbing out on to the roof, was relieved to see the rise of the waters slow. 'But where did it all come from? That stream's only a trickle.'

Hugh swung to look at her, his eyes as grey as the skies beyond the window. In cream shirt and trousers he looked bigger than ever. There was a slight stubble on his chin, softening the hard line of his jaw and his mouth was ominously thin.

'How do flash floods *usually* happen?' What a lovely familiar ring his sarcasm had. 'We've had seventeen inches of rain here in the past twenty-four hours— where do you expect it to go? There are floods all over the peninsula. The whole of Coromandel is cut off.'

'Is it?' Julia gulped. Thank God she hadn't known! 'I don't have a radio in the Beetle.'

The skin around the grey eyes twitched. 'Do you mean to tell me that you didn't *know*? Half of Thames is flooded! There are people trapped in homes and farms waiting to be lifted out by helicopter; the whole region has been devastated! You were out *there* . . .' he pointed, a savage jab, '. . . and you didn't *know*?'

'Why are we up here if the water won't reach the house?' Julia prevaricated nervously, her gaze skittering away from his intimidating hulk.

'Because the rest of the house is cold and covered with dust sheets,' he explained with steel-eyed patience. 'This house has been here over a hundred years, Julia. It's withstood floods before and I'm sure it'll withstand this one.'

Julia shivered, hoping for a little belated sympathy.

'Stand by the fire if you're cold,' she was told tersely. 'If you get pneumonia you only have yourself to blame.'

Julia put her hands out towards the blaze, thinking that one over. 'Look,' she said, trying to sound reasonable, 'so I took a little bit of a risk. There's no need to go on about it. I'm OK aren't I?'

'What in the hell are you doing roaming around on the loose anyway?'

As if she was a stray dog! Julia bristled. 'Looking for you of course!' she snapped.

He swore. 'You've come all the way from Auckland this morning?'

'Through hell and high water,' said Julia flippantly.

'Of all the stupid, irresponsible bitches!' He exploded, hands thumping on his hips as he strode across the room to tower over her. 'You must be a complete cretin! And why, for God's sake? What if I hadn't been here, what would you have done then? Gone straight back I suppose—probably driving to your death in the process!'

Julia muttered a sullen negative to the effect that she wasn't completely idiotic. 'I knew you were here because Connie told me.'

'So? No doubt she also told you when I'd be back in Auckland,' he shot at her.

'I couldn't wait.' Julia lifted her chin defiantly, her clothes beginning to steam along with her temper.

'You couldn't ...? God give me strength!' He grabbed her by the shoulders with a quick, jerky movement. 'You could have been *killed* out there you little fool.'

'All right, so I'm a fool, what else is new?' she flung at him. 'What are you so mad about? You would have been well rid of me wouldn't you!'

'Don't be so bloody childish!' He gave her a furious shake and then suddenly he wasn't shaking her anymore, but kissing her, crowding her close to his body, his mouth hot and hard on hers. For Julia it was bliss, vindication of all her doubts, but when she wriggled to come up for air, he let her go as if she was a hot coal.

'You can't stand around in those wet things all day,' he said hoarsely, backing away hurriedly as if the dampness was infectious. Julia stood open-mouthed, tingling all over from his delicious attack, her anger dissipating in delight at his nervousness.

'All my clothes are in my poor car,' she said faintly.

He frowned thunderously at her as she plucked at the

sweater where it held her breasts in wet embrace. 'Go and take a shower,' he ordered, in the manner of 'get thee behind me, Satan'. 'I'll see if Connie or the girls left anything.'

'What about hot water?' asked Julia, as he reached the door. 'Is there any power?'

'We've got a generator. That's what I was checking on down in the garage.'

Julia stood under a wonderfully hot stream of water, hoping he wouldn't find anything. She would look very sexy in one of his shirts—maybe irresistibly so, if he could be driven to kiss her when she looked like a drowned rat. She smiled dreamily at the tiled wall. He had been so *mad*. She had loved the way his teeth had gritted and his ears had flushed, the way his eyes shot silver sparks. The shell was *definitely* in imminent danger.

Wrapped in one of Connie's luxurious velvet robes, her clothes draped in front of the fire, Julia munched on toasted cheese sandwiches, eyeing Hugh as he sat in his chair, staring fixedly at the flames in the grate. They listened to the latest news and weather report on the radio through a veil of static. Coromandel was indeed cut off and on the verge of being declared in a state of emergency.

'Further rain, with isolated thunderstorms and easterlies up to gale force can be expected, decreasing slowly tonight,' finished the earnest young man from the Weather Bureau.

'Damn!'

'Looks like we'll be stuck here for a while,' said Julia, viewing his frustration with glee. 'You make a lovely toasted sandwich, Hugh, although you can't really fail with those griller gadgets. Don't you want yours?' She took his untouched share and wolfed them greedily—it was her first food since the chicken and champagne of the previous night. 'Umm, delicious,' she licked her buttery fingers. Hunger satisfied, it was time to go into battle. Much as she hated what she had decided to do, she really had no choice. Hugh was proof against propinquity alone.

'Seeing as we're going to spend hours and hours and *hours* together,' she said, settling more comfortably on the floor, 'what shall we do to amuse each other?' She blinked at him with wide, suggestive eyes and he over-reacted instantly, rearing up to his feet like an enraged bear.

'Damnit, Julia, if you came down here just to torment me . . .'

'Torment, *torment*,' Julia rose beside him, the red robe falling over her hands and trailing on the floor, so that she looked, to him, like a little girl dressed up in her mother's clothes. 'What an odd word to use, Hugh. Do I torment you?' She moved towards him, stumbling on the bunched hem of the robe and pitching forward conveniently into his arms. Body contact produced instant ignition. 'Oh . . . Hugh . . .'

'Julia, be sensible . . .' The rough plea brought forth a laugh, muffled in his crisp shirt-front. 'Sensible? Me? Who are you trying to kid? You've already impressed on me that I'm a fool. Let's be foolish together, mmmm . . .?' She snuggled against his chest, a tiny creature trying to nestle into his heart.

'No . . .' The word was dragged harshly from the depths.

'Yes.' She flung back her head to smile sensuously up into his rigid face. 'When are you going to stop fighting it? I want you and you want me . . . that's something you *can't* hide behind a poker face.' She pushed her hips provocatively against his to prove her point and he couldn't deny her the surge of his body.

Triumphantly Julia trailed her hands down the muscular arms to stroke up under his sleeves, finding the crisp hairs that curled down to his wrists, the inner tendons hard cords. He shook her hands away and she recklessly slid them up under his sweater, caressing the scalloped stomach, raking through the soft tangle on his chest. Virgin that she was, her body seemed to have taken on an instinctive voluptuousness of its own—flaunting, seducing, draining his physical resistance.

'I can show you a good time,' she attacked softly, at what intuition told her would be his weakest point. 'Richard said that I showed a lot of initiative in bed. He said I was . . .'

'Shut up!' Hugh swore at her, wrenching her hands from his body, holding them as, unwillingly: 'You said that you and Richard weren't lovers.'

'Did I?' she shrugged off the accusation and succeeded in producing what she hoped was a husky, rather than broken, laugh. 'Maybe I'm mixing him up with someone else. Now . . . who could it have been?' She tapped a finger against the serene curve of her cheek, mocking his silent outrage. She produced and discarded the list of non-existent lovers for his disapproval, watching his face grow more and more grim while his eyes began to burn blackly, bleakly, within their frosty rims. Recklessly she continued, surely the fire must melt the ice *soon*.

'You know, I think it *must* have been Steve,' she finished tauntingly, having seen how the mention of his brothers seemed to disturb him . . . perhaps he found that a little too close to home. 'Yes, *that's* who it was. He was such a lover . . . so raunchy and . . .'

'*Shut up!*' The savage whisper drilled out. 'I don't want to hear it, any of it. Just shut up! Shut up and get out. *While you can.*'

'Get out where? There's nowhere to go,' said Julia, taut with fear and expectation. 'All the roads are closed and there's a flood just outside the door. Neither of us can leave, we're both trapped. Why can't we make the best of it? Are you scared you won't match up to the twins? Worried about your Oedipus complex? Did nasty daddy turn you into a passive little mummy's boy? *God, Hugh——!*

The terrified cry was wrenched from her trembling lips as the mortally wounded bear rounded on her, raising enormous fists, massive body swaying, shaking, straining against the fatally weakened bonds of self-control. His expression was murderous, the veins in his temples standing out under the translucent skin, marking the slow, savage pulse of his rage. All Julia's instincts screamed at her to run, but she ignored them. *Love. Trust.* Hugh was teetering on the brink, as he had that day by the pool. This time her shove was utterly deliberate.

She caught one huge, shaking iron fist in her puny hand and wrenched it to her jaw.

'You want me to take it back? Make me! Go on, make me. Hit me, Hugh! Punish me. Make me say I'm sorry!'

She heard his tortured, inarticulate groan, felt the pressure of his knuckles hard against the frail bones of her face, felt all the crushing power of him, the blind, brutal strength.

'Go on, hit me. You know you want to. It'll make you feel good. Feel strong. Feel in control. That's what you want isn't it? Hit me, Hugh! Show me what a real *man* you are!'

He broke loose, swinging at her with a harsh, tearing sound, throwing the whole weight of his body behind the crunching blow. Julia half-sobbed, closing her eyes, waiting, dying, not believing.

She felt the shock of the violent airwaves and opened her eyes as his fist grazed her cheek and buried itself with a splintering crash into the wood panel behind her head.

'No . . . *no!*' With a grunting, anguished moan Hugh struck again, despairingly, *'Oh God!'* He stared sickly at the bleeding fist, an alien appendage, and the raw, splintered panelling.

'No.' His voice sank to a bloodless whisper of defeat, as if all his mighty strength had collapsed inwards on itself. The great head fell back, his eyes fanned shut against drawn cheeks and Julia was horrified by the glinting run of moisture along the roots of the long, dark lashes.

'No, no . . .' she echoed his moaning litany, putting her arms around the large, shockingly weak body, cradling it close to her warmth. She felt the depth of his despair in the racking shudders and tried to soothe him with her love. 'No, darling, never. You'll never, never hurt me. Love or hate. Never, not even in your blackest rage. We all know that you're incapable of it, those of us who love you. I'm so sorry, so sorry, I had to say those awful, ugly things. But I had to, darling, I had to show you . . . you're so stubborn, you would never have believed me . . .'

Slowly, painfully, his shudders eased and like an old man Hugh leaned stiffly away from her, far enough to see her tear-streaked cheeks, the pleading blue eyes. He blinked, and swore as the realisation came to him.

'You . . .?' He swallowed. 'You . . . did that on purpose?'

'I'm sorry,' she confirmed his dazed uncertainty. 'But you do see why, don't you?'

'You . . . took a risk.'

Her face illuminated with a gentle smile. 'I trusted you.'

The grey irises turned smoky as he stared down at her. 'On purpose,' he repeated softly. 'Yes . . . I do see. On *purpose*?' as if he still didn't quite believe it.

Julia waited, her heart thumping madly, schooling herself to patience and gasped as he reached out a casual hand and wrapped it around her throat, tightly enough to make the blood thrum unpleasantly in her head. 'Those things you said . . . about your lovers . . .'

'Lies. All lies,' croaked Julia.

'Lies.' He drew out the repetition delicately. 'My God! On *purpose*. I wanted to kill you. I *should* kill you.' His fingers flexed in the soft skin of her neck and she brought her own hands up to tug at them helplessly, trying to guess what was going on in that complex brain.

'But since you've just proved me constitutionally incapable of killing . . .' he dragged her towards him, '. . . perhaps there's another way I can give you a little taste of death.'

'What . . .?' Julia's knees sagged at the way he looked down at her body. There was a light in his eyes she had never seen before, a strange, unholy gleam.

'That's what they call it—*a little death.*' He reached down and loosened the voluminous robe, swiftly reaching behind her to pull it off before she had time to react. He still held her by the neck and the combination of helplessness and the startling realisation of what he intended to do sent a surge of confused excitement through Julia. Instinctively her hands came up to shield her unprotected body and he laughed, a relaxed, knowing laugh that stole away the last of her breath.

'Don't bother, Julia. Before I'm through I'm going to know every inch of you,' adding, to make her blush furiously; 'both inside and out.'

He kissed her possessively, removing his hand from her throat as her lips parted readily under his. He kissed her until there was no part of her mouth he had not sensuously explored. His large hands moved over her body, cupping and massaging her breasts with firm deliberation before sinking to her belly, and beyond, his fingers imitating the invasive stroke of his tongue in her mouth.

The flood outside was nothing to the seething waves of pleasure that flooded through Julia as she allowed Hugh the freedom of her body. He seemed without inhibition, as though he had shed the dry, constricting skin of his previous existence to emerge renewed and invigorated. Julia gloried in the return of his strength and power, arching as his hands found the naked skin of her back, tracing the sensitive curve of her spine urging her closer to his restless thighs.

Kissing, caressing, feeding hungrily on her soft flesh, Hugh's impatience was a seduction in itself, more arousing than all his previous expertise. He pulled off his clothes and threw them down, pushing Julia eagerly on to the floor in front of the dying fire, roughly entwining his body with hers, moving against her with a passionate urgency that consumed her with heat. The harsh-soft carpet beneath her and the heavy satin body above her provided her skin with a sensuous contrast that made her cry out with delight.

'So ripe, so ready,' he muttered, biting the smooth shoulders and breasts, then kissing the tiny, stinging pinpoints of pain, soothing them with his tongue, only to use his teeth again to skilfully heighten the sensations that were building . . . building, inside her body. He slid between her legs, one hand resting on the pulsing warmth of her left breast, lifting his head briefly, asking thickly: 'Am I going too fast for you?'

As Julia gasped a negative, he followed it roughly with: 'I don't care, we got all the damned foreplay over with months ago. *Now*. I've got to have you *now* . . .'

Julia arched herself to the thrust of his body, welcoming him joyfully into her warmth. She felt him tense momentarily at the moment of truth, beating down his desire as he met, then gently thrust through the fragile, unexpected barrier; his whispered moan mingling with her tiny cry. With the need for gentleness past, he exploded into impassioned lovemaking, bringing them both to a fierce, groaning satisfaction.

Afterwards, lying wrapped in the glow of fulfilment, Julia touched his mouth with a gentle finger.

'I was wrong. You did hurt me. But only a little.'

'If I'd known . . .'

'I'm glad you didn't,' not wanting a single regret. 'I wouldn't have wanted it to be any other way. And loving you made it perfect.'

He held her quiet gaze for long moments, then bowed to rest his chin against her bright head. 'Oh, Julia . . .

Richard was right to warn you. I'm too old, too selfishly staid for you. I can't live up to your expectations. Can't give you the kind of loving you deserve.'

Julia smiled secretly against his throat. His words held precious little enthusiasm, he wasn't even convincing himself any more. However, knowing his background, it was probably the nearest he would ever come to a declaration of love.

'Piffle,' she scoffed. 'Who's trying to be self-sacrificing now? Richard's been wrong before. So have you come to that, lawyer-man.' She tilted her head back to give him a cheeky grin. 'What was it you both said about lovemaking on the floor?'

For the first time Hugh seemed to take in their surroundings and to Julia's delight his ears went bright red. 'I'm going to ache in the morning.'

'So am I,' she replied mischievously. 'You're a very athletic lover. Very demanding.'

'Too demanding. No, listen to me Julia . . .' as she stroked him teasingly. His face was so beautifully grave that her heart was wrung anew with love and compassion. 'It's you I'm trying to protect, not myself. You're like a shaft of light in my life, all dancing brightness and warmth. All right, so you've satisfied me that I'm not my father's son, but there are other, just as bitter ways to cause pain. Our natures are diametrically opposed. You may love me now, but what happens when you find my rather pessimistic nature oppressive, what happens when you have to live with my wretched stuffiness day in, day out? I know you like to fly in the face of facts, but I don't have your rather awesome courage in that direction. You know I never would have come to you,' he said, with slow deliberation. 'I would have put all my considerable energy into convincing myself that life was better without you.'

'I know.' It didn't hurt. It was part of the way he was, part of the burden that she wanted to help him shoulder. 'But it wouldn't have been, would it? And I'm here now. I love you Hugh, and I know that you enjoy my company, you respect me, you make love to me with tenderness and passion. Isn't that enough to build a life on? A lot of people don't even start with that. As for your wretched stuffiness ...' she flicked him a provocative look '... I changed my mind about that the first time you kissed me. You're not stuffy, you're just out of practice in some areas.'

'Who told you about my mother and father?'

'Connie,' Julia answered warily, unsure of his exact mood. 'I went to *Romeo and Juliet* last night, and we talked.'

He nodded, heavy lids drooping. 'So, having had that over-tender heart of yours well-primed, you came hotfooting it down here to play the psychologist.'

Julia stiffened. 'So? It worked didn't it?' She dared him to accuse her of pitying, rather than loving, him.

'Extremely arrogant of you though, wouldn't you say?'

'Damn you, Hugh——' If only she knew what he was thinking!

'No, damn *you*!' he told her, with a forcefulness that was dismaying. 'I didn't want this, Julia. I didn't want *you*. I was quite content with what I had. But you changed that.' He looked at her anew. 'I should never have asked you to do my typing, but I couldn't leave well enough alone. You were so ... infuriating ... disruptive, so full of life, small yet fiery, warming everyone with your glow. I wanted to warm myself too, just enough to take the chill off, so I let myself be seduced by you ...'

'*I*? Seduced you?' squeaked Julia, wondering where all this was leading.

'You know you did.' His sombre face lightened with a smile that melted her bones. 'Always. In everything. With your big, baby eyes and your laughing mouth, with your impossible sense of humour and your tiny, accident-prone body. How could I not be fascinated? And you fitted into the palms of my hands as if that was where destiny intended you to stay. My God, how I wanted you that night ...' The memory lay physical hold of his body, and it stirred against her.

'Your love was one complication too many. It was too sudden, too soon, raising too many painful possibilities. I realised that with you it would have to be all or nothing, and I told myself it would be easier all round if it were nothing. Will you marry me? I know it won't be easy, but we can try.'

She almost missed it in the welter of doubting words. 'Yes,' she said quickly, before he could retrieve his error. 'Yes, yes, yes.' And, reassuring him with her honesty: 'And yes, I know it won't be easy, but often what's easy isn't worth a candle. We're different, but our differences are complementary. You can keep my feet on the ground and I can lift your head above the clouds. The whole world will be ours.'

'Ah, Julia ...' He drew her deep against his chest, a mixture of relief and resignation in the warm sigh.

She stroked his grey head. 'Before you settle in, perhaps you'd better go and put all this in writing. I really should tie you to a contract before you come back to your senses.'

'I don't want my sense back,' he said huskily. 'But you're right, we should draw a contract up, now. I feel an urgent desire to insert a rather pressing clause.'

His body nuzzled against hers and Julia giggled at the *double-entendre*. 'I never thought of laughter as erotic until I met you,' he murmured, catching her mouth with his own eager one. 'Do you think you can manage to do that while I'm inside you?'

'Hugh!' Julia wondered dazedly what manner of playful creature she had unleashed on to an unsuspecting world.

'I mean it. It's one of the many things I love you for.'

'Hugh?' Frantically Julia fought against his cleverly

roving hands, so that she could get a clear view of soft grey eyes. 'Hugh?'

He smiled, and the blood rioted through her body. She took a shaky breath. 'You devil!'

'I was saving the best until last,' he admitted. He watched the tears that glittered in her eyes with a curious, detached wonderment, not offering to kiss them away. She allowed him this piece of refined cruelty, even as she cursed him for it, for she understood the reason for the casual way he bestowed his unique gift. There were still fears that only a lifetime of loving could finally allay.

'You swine . . . you rat . . . you beast . . .' she sobbed.

'You love the beast in me, remember?' A gentle finger moved at last to brush away her tears. 'I can remember every word you've ever said to me. If I can forgive you some of your words, you can forgive me my lack of them. I had to be sure, first. I love you.'

'Oh!' Her head fell back and she shuddered with a kind of ecstasy that transcended the intense physical satisfaction they had shared.

'And now . . .' he returned to the matter at hand. 'I calculate that we have at least twenty-four hours before the phones are working and the roads cleared. I think we should use each and every one of them to our mutual . . . exquisite . . . advantage.'

'But, Hugh,' she gasped, as he picked her up and tossed her into the feathery depths of his bed as if she was but a feather herself. 'What about your work . . . you're supposed to be . . .'

'To hell with work,' his growl vibrated against her skin as he burrowed down alongside her. 'This is a civil emergency. It's our duty to support each other in time of need. Can't you feel how much I need you?'

Julia laughed and he laughed with her. Their joy rose to fill the quiet room . . . to settle there. How she always loved to hear him laugh!

Discover the new and unique

Harlequin Gothic and Regency Romance Specials!

Gothic Romance	Regency Romance
DOUBLE MASQUERADE	TO CATCH AN EARL
Dulcie Hollyock	Rosina Pyatt
LEGACY OF RAVEN'S RISE	TRAITOR'S HEIR
Helen B. Hicks	Jasmine Cresswell
THE FOURTH LETTER	MAN ABOUT TOWN
Alison Quinn	Toni Marsh Bruyere

A new and exciting world of romance reading

Harlequin Gothic and Regency Romance Specials!

Available in September wherever paperback books are sold, or send your name, address and zip or postal code, along with a check or money order for $2.25 for each book ordered, includes 75¢ postage and handling, payable to Harlequin Reader Service, to:

Harlequin Reader Service
In the U.S.
P.O. Box 52040
Phoenix, AZ 85072-9988

In Canada
P.O. Box 2800, Postal Station A
5170 Yonge Street
Willowdale, Ontario M2N 6J3

CR-A-1R

SPECIAL FREE OFFER

Janet Dailey

TREASURY EDITION

- *NO QUARTER ASKED*
- *FIESTA SAN ANTONIO*
- *FOR BITTER OR WORSE*

Now's your chance to rediscover your favorite Janet Dailey romance characters – Cord and Stacey Harris, and Travis McCrea.

Own three Janet Dailey novels in one deluxe hardcover edition. A beautifully bound volume in gold-embossed leatherette…an attractive addition to any home library.

Here's how to get this special offer from Harlequin!

AUGUST
TREASURY EDITION
COUPON

As simple as 1...2...3!

1. Each month, save one Treasury Edition coupon from your favorite Romance or Presents novel.
2. In four months you'll have saved four Treasury Edition coupons (only one coupon per month allowed).
3. Then all you have to do is fill out and return the order form provided, along with the four Treasury Edition coupons required and $1.00 for postage and handling.

Mail to: Harlequin Reader Service

RT1-A-2

In the U.S.A.
P.O. Box 52040
Phoenix, AZ 85072-2040

In Canada
P.O. Box 2800, Postal Station A
5170 Yonge Street
Willowdale, Ont. M2N 6J3

Please send me my FREE copy of the Janet Dailey Treasury Edition. I have enclosed the four Treasury Edition coupons required and $1.00 for postage and handling along with this order form.

(Please Print)

NAME _____

ADDRESS _____

CITY _____

STATE/PROV. _____ ZIP/POSTAL CODE_____

SIGNATURE _____
This offer is limited to one order per household.

SUPPLIES LIMITED

This special Janet Dailey offer expires January 1986.

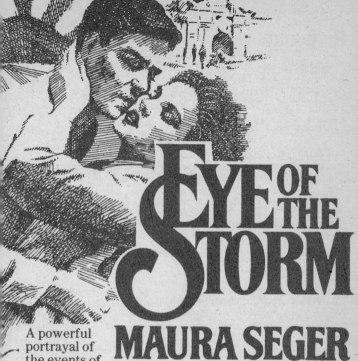

EYE OF THE STORM

MAURA SEGER

A powerful
portrayal of
the events of
World War II in the
Pacific, *Eye of the Storm* is a riveting story of how love
triumphs over hatred. In this, the first of a three-book
chronicle, Army nurse Maggie Lawrence meets Marine
Sgt. Anthony Gargano. Despite military regulations
against fraternization, they resolve to face together
whatever lies ahead.... Author Maura Seger, also known
to her fans as Laurel Winslow, Sara Jennings, Anne
MacNeil and Jenny Bates, was named 1984's
Most Versatile Romance Author by *The Romantic Times*.

At your favorite bookstore in April or send your name, address and zip or
postal code, along with a check or money order for $4.25 (includes 75¢ for
postage and handling) payable to Harlequin Reader Service to:

HARLEQUIN READER SERVICE

In the U.S.
Box 52040
Phoenix, AZ 85072-2040

In Canada
5170 Yonge Street
P.O. Box 2800
Postal Station A
Willowdale, Ont. M2N 6J3

EYE-E-1

You're invited to accept 4 books and a surprise gift Free!

Acceptance Card

Mail to: **Harlequin Reader Service®**

In the U.S.
2504 West Southern Ave.
Tempe, AZ 85282

In Canada
P.O. Box 2800, Postal Station A
5170 Yonge Street
Willowdale, Ontario M2N 6J3

YES! Please send me 4 free Harlequin Romance® novels and my free surprise gift. Then send me 6 brand new novels every month as they come off the presses. Bill me at the low price of $1.65 each ($1.75 in Canada)—an 11% saving off the retail price. There are no shipping, handling or other hidden costs. There is no minimum number of books I must purchase. I can always return a shipment and cancel at any time. Even if I never buy another book from Harlequin, the 4 free novels and the surprise gift are mine to keep forever.   116 BPR-BPGE

_____
Name   (PLEASE PRINT)

_____
Address   Apt. No.

_____
City   State/Prov.   Zip/Postal Code

This offer is limited to one order per household and not valid to present subscribers. Price is subject to change.   ACR-SUB-1

Experience the warmth of...

Harlequin Romance

**The original romance novels.
Best-sellers for more than 30 years.**

Delightful and intriguing love stories
by the world's foremost writers
of romance fiction.

Be whisked away to dazzling
international capitals...
or quaint European villages.
Experience the joys of falling in love...
for the first time, the best time!

Harlequin Romance

A uniquely absorbing journey
into a world of superb romance reading.

Wherever paperback books are sold, or through
Harlequin Reader Service

In the U.S.
2504 West Southern Avenue
Tempe, AZ 85282

In Canada
P.O. Box 2800, Postal Station A
5170 Yonge Street
Willowdale, Ontario M2N 6J3

**No one touches the heart of a woman
quite like Harlequin!**

R-111